D1052993

the Rendezvous

a novel

Justine Lévy

translated by **Lydia Davis**

Scribner

SCRIBNER
1230 Avenue of the Americas
New York, NY 10020

This book is a work of fiction. Names, characters, places, and incidents either are products of the author's imagination or are used fictitiously. Any resemblance to actual events or locales or persons, living or dead, is entirely coincidental.

Designed by Brooke Zimmer
Set in Caslon
Manufactured in the United States of America

10 9 8 7 6 5 4 3 2 1

Library of Congress Cataloging-in-Publication Data

Lévy, Justine.
[Rendez-vous. English]
The Rendezvous: a novel/Justine Lévy: translated by Lydia Davis.
p. cm.
I. Davis, Lydia. II. Title.
PQ2672.E948R4613 1997 97-3150
843'.914—dc20 CIP

ISBN 0-684-82579-1

Originally published in French as Le Rendez-Vous *by Plon*

for Isabelle D.

the Rendezvous

1

I'm the best thing mama ever did. At least that's what she claims.

"You're a miracle, my little miracle," she used to tell me in a fit of sadness.

The miracle wasn't me, or my name, or my face, but the happiness I reminded her of. The miracle was that I looked so much like the person she loved, the person who had left her. The miracle was that I lived on after their love was dead, that papa continued in me. It was that commonplace wonder—a father diluted in his child.

When she took me in her arms, she would study my face for a sign of his face, his smile, his glance. For a long time, she clung to these coincidences, to the ways we looked alike. Papa was still there in me. Through me, their lives were bound together, the splendor and misery of that love.

And then, it was my turn to leave her. I was seven years old, I had to get out, so I ran away, more or less. I know she felt it as a terrible defeat. And by leaving her that way I really think I lost her. How long has it been since she stopped holding me close to her heart? I miss it.

Her tenderness is somewhere else now. I perceive it from time to time, glimmers of it, in her laughter, on the telephone, in the way she wears her gray fox coat, the perfume in the fur. That perfume—is it the only thing I have left of her?

A message, yesterday, on my answering machine: "Hello, pet, I'm back from Kuala Lumpur, I have a lot of silly little things to tell you. Would you meet me at the Escritoire, in the Place de la Sorbonne, tomorrow at eleven? Kisses and hugs, my kitten."

"My kitten." Okay. Other people would say "my baby," "my angel," "my dear little girl," but she says "my kitten." The main thing is to get along with each other.

Right now she's late, as usual. I should be quite clear about this: Mama is a chronagnostic; time exists, but she doesn't believe in it. That's the way it is. However, she always feels the need to vindicate herself. So she makes up something, anything at all, as quickly as possible. She was pursued by a hired killer. Went to vote by proxy for an old aunt with a cold. Saved a cat from drowning. Didn't wake up. Went back to sleep. Took a sleeping pill instead of a vitamin. Was bitten by a lady in the post office.

When I was little I needed her lies, even if they hurt me. Now what discourages me is that I don't believe her anymore. So I pretend, because I'm so tired; she doesn't even bother to do a good job of lying anymore. What she says is always improbable, but she sticks by it.

Mama lies. There. It's her cure for depression, her remedy for the disease of feeling unimportant. Reality bounces off her, nothing matters: she smokes a joint at breakfast, forgets to have dinner, falls asleep on a bus.

"Oh, yes, pet, I know I'm strange—it's a sort of profession."

Last summer, on one of "our" Sundays, which we we were to spend together, we had a date to go visit some of her friends in Chartres. Mama was driving. Suddenly she made a right turn.

"This way looks nice."

"You're crazy!"

"I should hope so!"

In the end, we found ourselves back in Cannes. We never saw those particular friends again.

Once, just once, I asked her to explain it to me. How can a person live outside of everything, within a complete illusion?

"You know, my kitten, the illusion of happiness is always the happiness of an illusion. . . ."

Mama, the great sage in the presence of the Eternal.

The fact is, she will come. That's the most important thing: Mama always comes in the end. She'll order a draft beer, draw a heart in the foam with her finger. She won't drink it: The only thing she likes about beer is its color. I think I know her through and through. And yet how many times I've said to myself, seeing her arrive: That isn't her!

She's disarming.

She'll come, and when she enters the cafe, she'll attract every eye, and silence will fall around us.

2

I may as well say it: Mama is beautiful, very, very beautiful.

For a long time I contemplated her beauty in the eyes of the men who had anything to do with her. In those eyes I saw fever, a promise of danger. One day ten years ago, I came across a *Vogue* cover, one of the last she did before she went under, before she passed into that other life—the life of bohemian disorder which I feel somewhat responsible for and which has frightened me so since then.

I looked at her, that day, as though I were seeing her for the first time. Wait! That gilded statue, with eyes drawn out toward her temples—it was actually her! I stuck the photo above my bed, in place of Garbo, and I was paralyzed with admiration. That's my mama!

I saw how I could make use of the situation. I had already gone off to live with my papa. I didn't see her much. I filched her modeling portfolio, a large green file folder, and I methodically cut it to pieces. She reappeared projected on the walls of my bedroom all the way up to the ceiling: mama everywhere, in all four corners of the room, smiling at me and running toward me in a moiré bikini; mama in silver lamé and pearls with a Marlboro between her lips; mama in black and white behind a gate; mama on water skis, frothy waves all around her; mama staring at me with her large clear eyes; mama on a bicycle in the country; mama with a bottle of Chanel No. 5; mama half nude under the sun; mama in small pieces, her mouth on a bottle of champagne; mama in an evening gown in a bathtub; mama in profile, her nose so distinctly shaped.

Mama to the point of disgust, mama to the point of nausea. Mama looking at me at night, in the day-time, locked up with me inside those walls. But I missed her more than ever. Mama always there and yet so much somewhere else. I would reach out my arms to her and she wouldn't recognize me.

I returned her portfolio to her.

She wasn't disturbed even for a moment. "Well, well. You're already sick of it too."

She has changed since then; her beauty has—how should I say it?—melted into her face.

Men still like her, but she doesn't know how to love, so she simply warms herself in their rays and slips from one to another, indifferent. In fact, she isn't content with mere dreams or insincerities; she has a strong appetite, fed by a certain amount of scorn, and because of it she sees each man purely as an object to be consumed. It's a sad sort of gluttony, a sad sort of freedom. The appearance of love, the gestures, the music, but the sound is false: This is only playacting, and it always stops at the first act—there's an invitation to go on a journey, but no real journey. Above all, don't get really involved. Don't look back. Full speed ahead, stay completely detached.

Debauchery is fun, in the end. She exhausts her lovers, wrings them dry; they rarely last more than two months. Anyway, if they have the poor taste to become attached to her, even fall in love—the nerve!—she immediately gets rid of them.

I've finally realized that most of the time they're only pale stand-ins for papa. Small-time violinists, saxophonists of some kind, cabaret pianists, pop singers. . . . Obviously she could find someone better; but it wouldn't be right for one of them to take the place of her ruined love, or equal it or even—

sacrilege!—surpass it. That love floats over her, or else it springs up like a jack-in-the-box out of her head, and she's afraid of its sudden leaps.

She resents these men for being no more than what they are, for never being Him. What an odd pact, what a strange sort of loyalty. This mutilated life. . . .

And yet some time ago she got married again. Was she hoping for lightning to strike at city hall? The fact is, she and Alex didn't even spend their wedding night together and two months later they applied for a divorce.

I sometimes run across him in the Latin Quarter, where he still gravitates, and even now he seems stunned, clinging to the slightest scrap of memory. Exactly what happened? What obscure reasons drove this proud, talented man to let himself be duped like that, humiliated, dispossessed, trampled underfoot? Even he can't explain it. He doesn't hold anything against her. A few moments of grace, he says. The curious motions of her hand, easy and precise, when she was applying her blusher. The little girl in her. Her sharp profile. The distress in her eyes, the way her voice would break suddenly, the way she seemed to be saying "help me, rescue me," at the very moment she was kicking him out.

3

Why? Why did she let him go? Didn't she know that when she lost papa her happiness would vanish too and she wouldn't really be alive anymore? I've always told myself that some day I would try to find out. Some day it will be time for me to know, to understand.

Mama, my mama, I so much want to help you, let me help you, let me look out for you.

But mama doesn't hear, she has never wanted to hear, she won't allow anyone to be kind to her anymore. And anyway, what right would I have to be kind, since in my own way I abandoned her too?

Mama, so alone. So proud, and so alone. Time has stopped for her. The tortures she holds so dear. The ruins, the vestiges that haunt her endlessly. Now and then she wakes up with a start: There he is, he's coming back, she sees his long black coat in the distance. But now it's not him, it's never him wearing the coat. Then, alone in bed, or beside some transitory lover, she cries over the happiness she has lost.

Life goes on, of course, with its parade of pleasures and wild laughter. But there is resignation on her lips now.

From time to time, a fever: She consumes herself with alcohol, drugs, petty thievery, and as she wastes away, she watches with a certain sensuous pleasure, her eyelids heavy. Like a pendulum, she swings back and forth between sorrow and gaiety. Sometimes I'm frightened: Which side is she going to tumble out on?

Okay. Here I am, now, alone at the Escritoire almost twenty years later. Alone on this worn imitation leather, in this cafe where everything began. I've come back here today as though on a pilgrimage. This past doesn't belong to me, I'm attaching it to myself. These memories that occur to me, memories from which I no longer sort out what might be imaginary—are these her memories? Mine?

What an enigma it is that two people can love each other so much and then separate one day. And why isn't there a plaque by the entrance saying: "On this site, Alice D. and Aurélien H. first met"?

Indignation.

Her hennaed hair, the broad strokes of eyeliner under her light eyes, her manner like an angel, a fallen angel but more supreme than ever. I can hear her voice in the din.

Mama. My mama. I call her mama when I'm talking about her. But I call her Alice to her face because I want to let her know clearly how little the role suits her, how far beyond her it is.

Mama. Which of us is really the mother? Wasn't she the one who would forget to come pick me up in the rue Saint-Benoît when school let out, and wasn't I the one who would fill out her Social Security forms? Wasn't she the one who would shoplift—and she still does—as easily as she would sneeze, and wasn't I the one who would try to protect her? Oh, of course her maternal instinct wakes up sometimes. One year she decided, against my wishes, to go to a parents' meeting at school. She arrived there splendid but dead drunk. That was the day—I still blame myself for it—I told her she didn't deserve to be a mother.

I realize now that there is consistency in her inconsistency. The woman may be infinitely seductive, but the mother is dangerous. The important thing is to know this.

❀ ❀ ❀

My grandmother, Nany, was the first to discover the chaotic life mama had created for me. I was four years old. She was going down the rue des Saints Pères in her red Austin when, at the corner of the rue de Grenelle, a swarm of little barefoot gypsies emerged from a van singing bawdy songs at the top of their voices and crossed the street against the light. I was at the end of the line, a thumb in my mouth, decked out in an orange cape too big for me. Nany said nothing. But she took me by the hand and led me away to the other end of the world, to shelter, to a large apartment in the rue de Tilsitt. There, for a while, I tasted an antiseptic, warm happiness. Alice became mama again every Saturday at noon. I know she suffered too over this separation. Then, a little later, she enticed me back again—oh, not for very long!—into her great spirals of love and madness.

Great, Louise! Go on, be touched by your little life! But do you know where that leads? To sadness, nostalgia, which you detest. The image of yourself that frightens you so.

Well, what do you expect? Anyway, mama is coming. And when she gets here we won't talk about the past. No one ever talks about the past with her. She said she had "a lot of silly things to tell you," and I'm sure it's true, and I'm sure we're going to have a really good time.

4

Where is she coming back from? Oh yes, Kuala Lumpur. What did she go there for? Of course! One of her old girlfriends is in prison there for dealing heroin. Dear mama . . . so inconsistent about that too. Months go by and I don't hear from her, even though she lives eight metro stations away, and yet she's prepared to go to the end of the world to a bug-infested prison to visit Sophia who, I'm sure, doesn't care about her in the least.

Mama likes women too, and I've always taken that for granted. Even when I was very small, after papa left, I knew no one was supposed to hear about it except for a certain group associated with a feminist publisher at the time, and that it would probably be better if I didn't go and shout it from the school rooftop.

The situation didn't shock me too much. It didn't bother me as much as Sophia herself. Her twisted mouth, her stubborn expression, her strawlike hair. I talked to her as little as possible.

Sometimes, on Saturday nights, they would decide to go to the movies. When I didn't want to stay in the car—I was always afraid they wouldn't come back to get me—they would simply take me along. These were mostly X-rated movies—It's never too early to start educating children.

They would explain to the ticket seller: "She's only three, you don't think she's going to look at the movie, do you?" In fact, I would always end up going to sleep. But I still have strange images in my head, muddy and, fortunately, confused. Did mama think I was too little to understand? She wasn't wrong. But she wasn't taking into account my involuntary memory, that second memory, less innocent that she supposed. Now, I remember everything. And I understand. And I hold it against her.

❀ ❀ ❀

What time is it? Going on one o'clock. Already one o'clock!

"Waiter!"

"What would the young lady like?"

"What's your daily special?"

"Leek tart. But if I may, let me recommend the Auvergne stew. It's fantastic."

"I'd rather have the asparagus tart."

"Leek. I said *lee—eek!*"

"That's fine too. But quickly, please. I'm expecting someone, and the smell of leek isn't. . . ."

"I understand." (Knowing look.)

"I'm not sure you do." (Defensive manner.)

"One daily special! One!" (Look of someone who is not very pleased, who would really have liked to unload his Auvergne stew on me.)

Mama will be here any moment.

I hope she won't mind that I started without her.

Oh, come on! Here it is almost a year since I've had any news, everything's going very well for me, thank you, she takes off without saying a word, and on top of all that I should be willing to die of hunger! Has she any idea, even now, who I am? Will she recognize me? Has this young woman I've become kept the promises of her childhood?

Hello, madame, my name is Louise, I'm eighteen years old and I'm your daughter. I seem happy? The truth is, I am. Obstinacy or habit, I don't know anymore. In love? I have a lover, he's delightful and flatters my pride, but do I love him or his kisses? I'm demanding, and my loves are few and far between. The fact is, my heart is still a virgin and I'm waiting for Prince Charming.

What? No, you're right, I haven't really lived yet, but I'm in no hurry. Right now I've just passed my final exams, not without difficulty, and I need at least ten years of rest.

No thanks, I don't smoke. Oh, you're a palm reader? Look, see, it's odd, my life line is very short. Yours too? That's reassuring. Do you think that a tattoo extending it a little could influence my destiny? If you say so. . . . It's true, my heart line is long and sinuous, I hadn't noticed. I'll tell you something confidential: I think I'm in love with another guy. It's a new and interesting sensation. I met him at the little cafe in the rue Mangeclous one day when I was out on a lark with some girlfriends. A pale forehead under a tumult of brown curls. I hardly needed more than that. His name? The sweetest in the world. It reverberates in me, it makes me dizzy. He's called . . . I call him . . . Adrien. No, we haven't spoken yet. Yes, I have a romantic temperament and I need a nebula of stars around me. Oh dear, mother of mine, will I have to feel this emptiness some day too, this abandonment and heartbreak? Has the experience of your despair made me wary of love and its acts of destruction? I've read a lot, you've cried a lot, but my faith is intact, and I'm sure a day will come when I will look into Adrien's eyes and see eternity.

We'll talk about it some more, mama, since it interests you. But only if you get here soon. Girls in love can't wait forever.

Two hours late already! What are you up to? What excuse will you invent this time?

I could call you, of course. But I don't really know where you live anymore.

I'm not sure you know either. You've always despised comfort, you've always made it a practice to be late with the rent. You sleep here, there, in some guy's place, some woman's place, with an Argentine lover or a pal from the clink, in an elegant bed-and-breakfast or a squat in Vincennes.

You don't care, you cover your tracks, you lose yourself, it makes you laugh. And what about me, in all this? Do you think I'm laughing?

And what if she doesn't come at all?

Deliberation.

Heads yes, tails no. But if it's tails, it's heads, to ward off bad fate. And if it's heads, it's heads, no question. So it's heads. I knew it. She couldn't not come. But then why isn't she here yet?

5

This emptiness around me, the emptiness of everything that isn't her. And yet the earth turns, turns, never stops turning even when we don't see each other for a year. All these people here, who live, who breathe, who sweat, who are also waiting, maybe. This compact, blurred mass of people having their lunch. There's nothing startling here, nothing particularly outstanding.

Okay. Stop thinking about her. Pay a little attention to the rest of them. That woman over there who's flirting, the poor thing, her hair tangled in hairspray, she must think she looks pretty good. The other one, opposite, her receding chin, already dissolving into her neck. That guy at the bar, his confident look, his nose like a snail shell. Those students ordering steak tartare good and spicy or iced coffee and telling smart adolescent jokes: Restrain your ambitions a little. *Puff puff puff.* Or talking about literary soap operas: Proust was jilted, his aristocratic pal Montesquiou got into a fight. Who cares about them! Can't you see—mama isn't here, it isn't right, something has happened to her and Louise is crazy with worry? This girl here in front of you who's pretending to daydream but really wants to cry. Can't you see I'm not feeling well and I'm going to faint?

"And who is the nice leek tart for?"

"For me, thank you."

"Here you go! Be careful, it's hot."

"Can I have some pickles and ketchup?"

"Ketchup? With my leek tart?"

"Yes."

"Young people today!"

"She has *always* loved ketchup."

"What do you mean 'she'? Isn't the tart for you?"

"Never mind. You'll understand. She'll come and you won't even think about your ketchup anymore."

The taste of ketchup. Another thing I owe to her. She always says: "No meal without color, no meal without ketchup." All right! I'm going to eat up half the dish. Maybe that will make her come quicker.

There, you see? Finally! Just what I said: Here she is. Her long belted coat. That profile, with the light behind it—I would recognize it among a thousand others. Mama. Dear mama. You see, you were right about ketchup, it goes with everything.

Poor dope! Sit down again, quick. It's only Amélie. To confuse mama with that idiot who thinks she's a star just because she posed twice for *Jeune et Jolie.* I'm furious. I hate her. Daring to imitate mama. Taking advantage of the fact that I'm nearsighted. And on top of that, I know her: She'll be so proud that I stood up and said hello that she'll attach herself to me for an hour. Sound the retreat. Take cover. There's that look on her face, the starlet look that says excuse-me-for-having-made-you-wait-excuse-me-for-being-so-beautiful. If only I could get out of here, hide behind my leek tart. Too late.

"Hello, Louise, what are you doing here?"

"I'm waiting for a friend."

"And you're having lunch without waiting for her?"

"She's anorexic."

"Who is it?"

"You don't know her."

"That would surprise me, I know everyone. . . ."

"Her name is Epaminondas."

"Epa . . . I don't understand. I never heard of her."

"I guess not."

"You know what? Something stupid happened to me. I have to tell you."

"Just give me the gist, please."

"I had to pass an oral in ancient languages with Monsieur Schmirtz. Can you see it? I go into Richelieu Hall. Walking like a model, of course. But completely on edge. I go up, and I say—listen to this—"Can I *sat* down?"

"I see . . ."

"And you know what he answers, the bastard? He says, 'No, but you can *gone* out.' "

"So you gone out?"

"Yes. I don't have to tell you that's not going to be the end of it!"

"Right, Amélie, look, I have to . . ."

"But here I am talking my head off, and you haven't told me a thing about yourself! You know what people are saying? I don't know if I should tell you. . . . But after all, you're my friend, you have the right to know."

"Nice of you."

"They say things aren't so great between you and David anymore. Well, I stick up for you, I say no, Louise isn't like that, it's not her way to cheat on her lover."

"Thanks."

"But you can tell me. Is it true? Are you cheating on him?"

"Excuse me, I'm going to finish my ketchup tart, the leeks are getting cold."

"Tell me! Tell me!"

"Can you keep a secret?"

"I'm silent as the tomb."

"Well, yes, I *am* cheating on him."

"I knew it. Who with? Olivier? Manu?"

"Sebastien."

"Wait. Sebastien. . . . The English prof? No-o-o!"

"No. Sebastien. . . . Monsieur Seb. . . . Your father! But keep quiet about it, okay? It's been going on for two months."

"I . . . I don't feel very well . . . I think I have to go. . . ."

"Want some leek tart before you go?"

"Thanks anyway. I can't stay. It's late. I'm off."

Phew. Rid of her. What a nobody! Still, while we were talking I wasn't thinking about mama, the fact that she's not here, her carelessness.

Tell the poor thing to come back? "Hey, kid, it was a joke!" Oh, I guess not. That girl is really too idiotic.

Pick somebody up, maybe?

That guy over there, by himself, who's been staring at me for a while now.

He's not bad. Tell him? "Hey, you, Marcel, yes you, moron. You know you're really cute!" And then what? Go to his place, let him kiss me, touch me. . . . His big hands. That beard! Better stay here and wait for mama.

Mama! Mama! Come on! Get here! Faster! Do people keep their daughters waiting like this for hours? Is that what you were taught in your life? Well, that's nice! Forty years old, and still not capable of changing the battery in her watch or taking the metro without making a mistake. Babies get lost! Damn, damn, damn!

There I go. Sad again. And without any warning, as usual. Maybe I lack certain vitamins, magnesium, trace elements. Trace elements are important. I don't know exactly what they are. But they must be important, since mama swallows them every morning before her first cigarette. She smokes four packs a day. No, not packs of trace elements—cigarettes. How does she manage to smoke so many? Just a matter of willpower, she says. It's quite simple, she lights the new one from the butt of the old one and she wakes up in the night to have a smoke. She always says: "I need a smoke."

And what about me—doesn't she need me?

Does she wake up in the night to call me: "My pet, just one kiss, a little kiss on your forehead. Sleep well, my baby, sweet dreams"?

Does it matter to her at all, how she hurts me all the time? Did she used to think of me when she passed a child in the street? And now, a girl who looks like me?

Is she on her way? Is she going to come, in the end?

She is my mother, that's certain. She brought me into the world: For that, at least, I'm grateful to her. As for the rest. . . . Oh, the rest! I have finally understood.

Bitter? One would at least have to be bitter. Does she know how sad I am? Does she realize that every morning I wait for a letter from her and it doesn't come? Does she know that when she forgets my birthday, she steals ten years of my life away from me? And then there's also this: What wicked pleasure does she take in blackening my image of her?

This stifling rage, sometimes.

I grow to hate you from loving you so much, mama.

I wish I would never hear another word about you.

How egotistic, and hard, and careless you are! But then again, you're also wonderful, delicate, enchanting. Your velvety voice, your hair floating over your shoulders. Sometimes you plan a treat for me—you take me to the movies. Surprise. Gaiety. How we love each other then! This is drama. This is tragedy. This is why I suffer and why there's nothing I can do about it.

6

And then there's this scene. The most atrocious time I've ever had to go through and one that will be here, inside me, I'm sure, to the very end.

Maybe it sounds melodramatic when I say it like this: But that morning I saw my mother die and come back to life in my arms.

That sharp pain now. . . .

That burning, here, all the time. . . .

Even here, in this cafe where I ought to be so cheerful since I'm waiting for her and I know she's going to come.

Something died in me that day, something I prized more than anything else—maybe an ultimate ingenuousness.

I'm fifteen years old.

A photographer from a small modeling agency has taken some snapshots of me, I've just received them, I don't recognize myself, I deduce from that that they're terrific. Quick, show them to mama, she'll be so proud.

Zip zip I run, zip onto the bus, zip onto the metro, zip Abbesses, zip rue Lepic, quick the code, 3604, the three stories, four steps at a time, I don't know yet that I'm climbing them for the last time.

Tralala, life is beautiful, mama, it's me, surprise! Hey, I never noticed: She put both our names on the door. But I hardly ever come here. . . .

I ring, no one answers.

"Mama, look, me too, fashion photos, black and white, pointed shoes, lipstick!" I yell. I hammer on the door. Maybe she's still sleeping. At noon? Yes, of course! At noon! I hammer again. Still no answer. I say to myself: "I'm going to leave." I don't leave. I glue my ear to the lock. I hear Belle-Lurette, the Siamese, meowing. I ask through the door: "Belle-Lurette! Belle-Lurette! Where is she, where's Alice?"

The neighbor on the landing pokes her head out, looks me up and down, and mutters something before slamming the door. I catch the echo of a curse, I pretend to ignore it. I'm so happy. A little disappointed, but so happy.

I take the photos out of their envelope. Do I look like her? She was the one I was thinking of when the photographer said to me: "Smile, look at me, dance!"

I'm going to put them under the doormat, with a little note. Darn, nothing to write with! Never mind, no little note. But under the doormat I find the key. Fabulous! I'll wait for her inside, she'll be so pleased!

First, there's an acrid smell that makes me gag. Then the usual nauseating disorder. The shutters closed. It's dark, and damp. I look around. I see clothes thrown on the bed. On the floor, a man's hat. On the walls, everywhere, photos of me as a baby, enormous, bald, horrible little monster. I have lovelier ones now, lovelier photos—you'll see! And then, in the corner close to the radiator, there's mama—but is it really her?—lying on the floor completely naked, curled up into herself. She's asleep.

I don't understand. Why on the floor?

I whisper: "Mama? Mama?"

I go closer. She's not curled up, she's crumpled up, prostrate.

I rush forward, I trip. Have I hurt her? I don't know. There's blood everywhere.

I kneel down. Cadaverous, her eyes half open, turned up toward the sky, she moves a little: twitches, shivers. . . .

I lean closer, I brush her hair out of the way, that long, golden-red hair I've always been so proud of. Mama? What's the matter, mama? Answer. What have they done to you, mama mama mama! Her forehead is lacquered with sweat, a thread of spittle running down from the corner of her mouth.

I put my hand under the back of her neck and lift her head. I tap her on the cheek. Her cheek is so cold, suddenly. Wake up! Open your eyes! And then I notice a blood-spotted scarf knotted tight around her pretty arm, which is blue from the network of veins. And then, next to it, the syringe.

I close my eyes. I must have made a mistake. Not her, not here, not today, not mama! The earth moves, pitches under my feet. I stumble, I cry out, I mutter some incoherent words. And then I am filled with rage. I look at her again with anger, disgust. And I slap her. A hard slap, almost a punch. Now I hit her with my fists, I kick her, I can't stop myself from hitting her, and I insult her: "You're revolting, disgusting, how could you have done this, I hate you!" I hate her, this woman I don't know, this stranger who is dying in front of me, who no longer feels anything, who doesn't react. She is soft under my blows, mama, my little rag doll. . . .

I lie down next to her, I untie the tourniquet, I take her in my arms, I kiss her neck, her swollen eyelids, her nose, I rock her, "Mama, mama, my mama, my dearest, my little girl, wake up, wake up. I'll never leave you again, we'll stay together forever." A tear rolls down her closed face. Her eyes blink, open, irises the color of rain, her eyes are wet, gazing into herself.

"Mama, look at me, I'm here, it's over. Here . . . come on."

One last spasm, she is trembling now.

"Mama, you're all pale." I take her hand, her delicate hand also striped with little blue veins. Then a sigh comes out of her, like a hiccup, hoarse, almost a rattle, she says "no, no" in a voice that comes from very far away.

The telephone, quick, where's the phone, there it is, under a pile of old newspapers, hello, hello, why doesn't it work, the stupid thing, come on, try! The bill, of course. She must not have paid the bill. I heave the thing against the wall, where it smashes with a jangling metallic noise.

Disturbance outside. The neighbor exclaims: "This racket is intolerable! Never a moment's peace! Gang of degenerates!" She rouses the building. She goes away and calls the police.

Then everything becomes hazy. I think a long time goes by. I have no idea. It's so distant. I'm there, on the floor, crouching next to this woman with her waxen face, with her hard features. This woman who is also my mother. This woman I talk to gently in the dark, and who doesn't hear me.

How could I have stayed so long talking to her without her hearing me? How could I have stayed so long without knowing her? I would give twenty years of my life not to have experienced that. I'm almost twenty years old. I would give my life.

She's there, in my arms, heavy, sprawling. Nothing else exists in the world. What do I feel? Nothing. Anesthesia of the senses. The cat comes and rubs against my leg, purring. Stupid animal.

She stayed in the hospital for a week. I wasn't allowed to see her. She was the one who didn't want it. She didn't want to endure my gaze, my pity, my grief. Then they took her to Garches. There was a message on my answering machine: "You'll see, pet, they'll make me explosively healthy again."

We never talked about that incident again. I still ask myself—and I don't get an answer—who was that woman, that stranger in her? How could I have seen nothing coming, felt nothing? No sign of that despair? No indication? Those images of her said it all, but I didn't want to listen.

I still don't want to. I'm so close to the edge of things. There's such a stifling fear in me. I'm almost never willing to remember that horrible morning. I have to be here, at the Escritoire, with nothing to do, in front of the "pickle extra" the waiter has just brought me, to think about it again like this. And I feel miserable.

These days? Oh, she certainly must start up again from time to time, when the first tremors of melancholy appear. What do they call it? Oh yes, a little "fix." Alex told me she would inject herself in the gums, to avoid bruises. It's monstrous, but I don't really care. There or somewhere else. . . .

❀ ❀ ❀

At this point, I may as well try to see things the way they are. I've been here, thinking about her, for two hours now. Because what else are you going to think about, when you haven't seen your mother for months, she's late, you're waiting for her, and you don't dare ask yourself: How will she act when she comes in? What will she say? What will her first words be?

That miracle of a body on which neither unhappiness, nor time, nor injections into the gums seem to have any effect: I'm anxious, yes, but I know that she will be, as always, insolently beautiful.

So I'm thinking about mama. I let my memories pour out, torment me. And . . . how can I say it? Forgive me, mama, but here it is: What comes to the surface, what stays inside me, mostly, is nothing but pain. Didn't we also have some really nice, affectionate times? Yes, of course. But my memory, you see, isn't very tactful. And I think I've forgotten those times.

Now and then, it's true, a moment of clarity. She's next to me in the bus, she's talking to me, she laughs, she makes fun of the guy opposite, who's all shriveled up. She gestures broadly, she begins to sparkle, she asks me questions, takes an interest, gives me advice, returns to the guy, laughs again, laughs at everything, we're so happy to be there, so happy to be together. And then all of a sudden, that veil in front of her eyes, that fever in her gaze, the wind of madness that comes—a few more seconds and it will be over; the moment of grace will have slipped away; mama won't be there any longer; she'll go on talking, her legs crossed, next to me, in her gray silk suit, with her jasmine perfume, but it won't be her anymore, she'll look at me without seeing me.

She brushes against me. She's already gone. Take me along, mama, take me along. That's the way mama is. She never takes me along, it's too far, too dangerous, she knows very well that you never come back from there in one piece. This lasts five minutes, or an hour. For an hour she is there, alive, and then she disappears.

Mama, like an eclipse.

7

One day not very long ago, she decided I should live with her again. It was early in the year, I was about to turn sixteen. For exactly nine years we had been "separated."

She came to meet me in front of school, in a lime-green suit, flat shoes, hair rolled into a bun: "Pet, we have to talk." And then she continued very fast, without stopping, chaotically: "You're my little girl, my child;

children should live with their mothers, that's the way it is, and it's a wonderful thing."

I'm surprised, of course. Those words colliding: "I've changed, you know, I've matured. I've become responsible, I earn money every month, a lot, we'll spend it. Come on. We'll live in a pretty apartment that I've rented by myself in the rue du Bac. There's a room for you, with a sunny terrace, we'll grow flowers there, vegetables, whatever you like. I've begun to decorate it the way you like. I've bought some shag carpets, the same as when you were little. And a goose featherbed. And a big wooden desk. I'll entice you. We'll have cherry bubblebaths and chocolate strawberries."

I want to laugh: "Mama, I'm not five years old anymore!" But she repeats it again, "come on, come on," like a broken record. "You'll be able to have your friends over, plan parties on the weekends, I'll lend you my hats, I'll let you smear my lipstick on the mirrors. It'll be like before, only better. Come on."

My friends Delphine and Tatiana are walking by on the sidewalk across the street. Do they recognize mama? They've only seen photos of her, on the covers of old magazines or in books. But out of the corner of my eye I see that they're thunderstruck by the spectacle. Mama is talking very quietly, but with a lot of animation. I look contrite, guilty. "Louise is getting a scolding," they must be saying to each other. "She's sixteen, and she's being scolded like a child."

I signal discreetly with my hand. They go off.

Mama continues: "My life is stable now, I get up in the morning, I'll help you with Latin and English, it'll be fun. Come on. Come on. In the evening while we make supper, we'll sing the songs you used to like. You remember? That song Jeanne Moreau sang. . . ."

Did I remember! Mama always puts on the same record over and over again fifty times in a row, until it tears my soul apart, until I cry for mercy. "I like the way you taste, you're sweet, Léon; but you're not much to look at 'cause your hair's too long. . . ." All day long, "Léon, Léon." In her bath, "Léon, Léon." On her bicycle, "Léon, Léon, Léon. . . ."

"Come on, darling, we'll be happy, you'll see, I'll be your mama at last, that's what it's all about, my life, my goal will be to take care of you, your happiness, your homework. . . . We'll have time just for us, we'll put honey cream on our hair and we'll watch *Barry Lyndon* on the VCR. And *Midnight Express.* We'll go for long rides through Paris on our bicycles. Come on, my little love, my baby, come on. I'm sure Belle-Lurette misses you, I bought her for you, after all. I've done some stupid things, but I've calmed down, I've thought a lot about it, you have to come back, you're my child, my little girl, I love you, come on, we'll play jokes on the telephone the way we used to. Come on, my dear, my little tiny child, come on. Let's try it. Give me a week, just one week. We'll make up for lost time, all those years of craziness. Come on, come on."

There, it's over. Her face is radiant. She takes me

in her arms. I'm taller than she is, so I lean over and snuggle against her. She pushes me away a little, lifts a lock of hair that has strayed over my eyes, looks at me with gratitude. All the things she has never been able to say to me, all those repressed words, the tenderness she has kept from me. . . . I'm not her little kitten anymore, I'm her child. Her sixteen-year-old child. Today, in front of the school, she realizes she's a mother and she has a child.

I dissolve in tears. She thinks I'm crying for joy and hugs me even tighter.

She heaves a long sigh, an interminable sigh of satisfaction, of liberation. And I wish I could disappear.

There I am, pressed against her. Her breathing has become regular again. I close my eyes. And what I see is my father: I owe him so much, he has watched me grow up, he has never stopped loving me, every day, at every moment, and she is asking me to leave him.

I want to run away. Find papa, the happiness she wants to shatter. I should say this to her: "You don't have the right. You can't. What you're asking me to do is crazy, and wicked, and senseless, you know that very well." But her joy terrifies me. And I can't think of a word to say.

My pain and her happiness become confused. She grasps my face in her hands, our tears mingle, she looks at me without seeing me, she looks at me from farther off, and I say to myself: "She'll understand, she must understand, my life is with papa, calm and safe, with Schubert, Purcell, Botticelli, lunch at one o'clock, dinner at eight, piano lessons, dance lessons, literary discussions, a contagious happiness, that diffuse feeling of bliss. Don't you see—it's all over, it's too late, the time when I needed you, your warmth, your tenderness, was before? Don't you sense that my place is with him, in clarity and gentleness? Your delinquent pals, your temporary mistresses, the always-full ashtrays, the unmade bed, that morass of confusion. . . ."

And then I'll say to her: "This doesn't mean I can't love you. I'm proud of you, I need you, but if I left it would break papa's heart and mine too."

And yet I don't say anything. Lost in her state of bliss, she wouldn't hear me. She would refuse to hear. And then there's also . . . how should I put it . . . that odd little fear, or that cowardice, yes, that's what it is, a cowardice that comes from the depths of my childhood, that always helped me survive but now condemns me.

I don't dare look at her. She thinks it's emotion.

I manage a wretched smile. She thinks: "A smile of happiness."

I can't say anything to her. She thinks it's because I want to listen to her.

She goes on, even more outrageous, she talks to me about vacations by the sea, shopping, new girlfriends I'll make, excursions in the car, we'll organize some *corridas,* we'll ride horses in the pampas, we'll go back to Saint-Malo, Mexico and Java.

I've stopped listening. I don't want to hear any

more. My eyes are half closed. I wish I were somewhere else. Or someone else. I wish I had the courage to confront her disappointment, her sadness, her little dream put to flight. I know what I should say. But I have a lump in my throat. And I'm afraid. And also I feel so tired. I try to smile one more time. And I cry and cry.

She hugs me even harder, whispers the sweetest words of consolation in my ear. And I hear myself say to her, in a voice I hardly recognize: "Wonderful. This is wonderful. I'm so glad."

She: "Is it true? Is it really true? You'll come?"

I: "Yes, it's really true."

One last time, shaking my head like a robot, I try to signal no. But she thinks I'm saying yes. Maybe it really is yes, in the end. Two days later I'm at the rue du Bac.

8

I remember everything. Day by day. Almost hour by hour.

What time is it, anyway? Two-fifteen. She's going too far.

I'm bored. If only I had a book. I knew she would be late. Mama is bound to be late and I didn't bring a book.

So, I remember everything. Those pictures of us at the rue du Bac. I'm going to recall everything. And when she gets here, I'll tell it all to her.

I know her so well, I'm sure she remembers too, but her version won't be the same.

When I was little, she was quite capable of becoming angry at me when I told her that Vercingetorix was defeated by Julius Caesar. She would say: "No, pet. I don't agree. Not Caesar: Augustus, or Caracalla, or Flagada." I would say to her: "But mama, you can't agree or disagree, that's the way it is, it's in the encyclopedia." She would persist: "Yes, but I don't agree."

A season with Alice, then.

Minutes of the season.

Agree or disagree, it will still be better than staying here without doing anything.

A coffee? No, no coffee. I'm fidgety enough as it is. A strawberry milk instead, to put me in the mood.

So, Monday, rue du Bac. There's a smoothie in the kitchen for breakfast and Mama—my mama the fury, my mama the glamour-girl—is preparing an eggplant gratin for dinner. The scene is surprising but rather convincing.

Tuesday. Same mise-en-scène. Perfect mother. She's there when I come home from school, she's sewing a button on my blouse, her forehead creased, completely absorbed in her work, thrusting her tongue out of her mouth like a diligent schoolgirl. She scarcely looks at me but smiles beatifically, radiant, so proud, this ex-magazine pinup, this extravagant, disorderly creature. Oddly, I'm bothered by it. I'm almost ashamed, suddenly. Then she says to me, in a protective tone I haven't heard her use before and that hardly suits her: "Hi, Louise, sweetie! Good grades today? Do you have much homework? Can I help?" and I can't help it, I burst out laughing. There, now, she's annoyed. Her stubborn pout. Her closed face. As though I had broken something. She's making me feel a little bad. After all, she's going to so much trouble to seem like the real thing.

So I have to restrain myself. Kiss her on the forehead. Play my part in the comedy too. It's my turn to protect her. Almost randomly, I blurt out: "I need your help. The math teacher's making a stink, he thinks I cheated on the last oral. Could you go see him?" Mama is reassured. A proud little smile. She says she'll think it over. That's it, think it over, I'd love to see Monsieur Trochu's expression when he sees you arrive in a crimped dress with broad gold stripes and your ivory cigarette holder at eleven in the morning.

Everything is going well. We're saved. The important thing isn't that I should be happy with her but that she should think I am.

Wednesday. Miracle. She's still playing her role. She's even beginning to impress me. Could it be that she has really changed? She has prepared a large omelet filled with a heap of complicated things—

mushrooms, tomatoes, salmon. I say: "Hey, there's quite a crowd in this omelet!" A month earlier, she would have laughed. Now she isn't laughing. She must think a mama doesn't have time to laugh. Too bad. Because I'm fed up with giving her her cues. I'm beginning to miss Alice.

Thursday. I go off to school. She isn't awake. I come home for lunch, and she's still in bed. The atmosphere is more relaxed. I point this out to her. I shouldn't have. Now she's frowning. "I have a right to a little time off, don't I?" Yes, of course! How can I tell her? I think I prefer this.

Friday. She didn't sleep here. Fine. Life is returning to normal. That evening, a gang of stupefied born-again hippies come and camp out in the apartment. This is beginning to interest me.

Saturday morning. Impossible to breathe. You can smell hash all the way out on the landing. I stumble over one weirdo sleeping in the living room doorway, I wake up another snoring in the bathtub, I can't find my toothbrush, little blackened spoons are lying here and there in the kitchen. Drugs are boss again, and they're taking her away from me. Endgame. Didn't I predict this from the first day? I go back home, find papa quite unsurprised, he didn't believe for a moment that things would turn out any other way. Poor mama. Weren't the dice loaded?

Wasn't the deck stacked? As usual, she bets all she has. But she lost the habit of winning a long time ago. Mama the daredevil, mama the fanatic.

Even so, we lasted almost a week. Quite an accomplishment. Generally as early as the second day, one of us would have burst into tears.

Most of the time, it was me. Her lack of faith had a way of exasperating me: It wasn't only Vercingetorix's victory, it was also Charlemagne's coronation, and Napoleon did not die at Saint Helena, Molière was not Molière, there are lipids in oranges, white wine doesn't make you as drunk as red. And when she took me for the weekend, when I was younger, we would both get into a bad temper before long. My physics problems were impossible, mama was out of cigarettes, she had received an outrageous bill, the bakeries were closed on Sunday, there was nothing on TV, it was too cold, too hot, I had left my raincoat at papa's. In short, life was wretched. She would lock herself in the bathroom. I would put Cat Stevens on with the volume turned as high as it would go. We would end up calling each other every name in the book, and I would leave the apartment and slam the door behind me. So much for you, you're so mean, I'm never coming back, I swear it.

Usually I would wait at the bottom of the stairs for five minutes—an eternity. I would cry a little. Really, I'm so cruel to her! And when I guessed she had suffered enough, I would go back up as fast as my little legs could carry me. Just in time, I thought, to stop her from calling the police. "Help! Help! My daughter Louise has run away!" I would find her in her bedroom, peacefully trying on an aluminum-colored wig or completely absorbed in painting her nails. "Okay, have you calmed down now?" I would bark. She would laugh at that and we would make up, and play a game of backgammon. Indulgent, I would always let her win.

9

That woman with her back to me—that could be Her. Oh no, I won't fall for that again! No one's going to repeat what Amélie did to me. The light isn't as bright now. No more backlighting. No more misunderstandings. But the same silky hair, the same regal way of holding her head. And she has her cigarette in her left hand too. Her long fingers I can imagine. It's Her, and it's not Her. She would like to be Her, of course: Is there any woman in Paris—especially in the place de la Sorbonne—who wouldn't dream of being Her? But this particular one isn't even close, the poor thing, and any second now I'm going to see that she doesn't even begin to compare. Is it normal, at my age, to go on believing your mother's the most beautiful woman in the world? And is it normal to be disappointed over and over again?

For a long time I had the same nightmare every night. I arrive at the Vavin, the cafe where we're supposed to meet, at noon on Saturday after school lets out. Wonder of wonders! Mama is there, she's waiting for me, early for the first time. She's sitting there in her gray fox coat, her little gold compact resting on the table. I run toward her, I bump into people, sorry, sorry, excuse me, sorry, and then, slowly, very slowly, it seems to take all night, she turns around. I see her classical profile, the vein that beats at her temple. And then suddenly I blink my eyes: It isn't mama anymore, it's a horrible woman, Snow White's stepmother, she has a long nose covered with warts, hair on her chin, no teeth, and with a hideous smile she says, "Kiss me, my love." I'm rooted to the spot, I can't move, it's an evil smile, a kind of rictus; I say to myself, "No, Louise, you're asleep, come on, your mother's beautiful," I slap myself, I pinch myself, but the woman is very close to me now, she smells of wine, she opens her eyes wide, two gaping holes, and I wake up, feverish and soaked in sweat.

For months this nightmare tormented me. I didn't want to sleep anymore, I would drink liters of Coca-Cola before going to bed, I was numb with exhaustion during the day, my grades went down, I cried all the time. And then abruptly, it went away.

My first attack of reading bulimia took place at about this time. I was nine years old. I thought you had to be twelve to be a "big" girl, wear jeans, take buses, elevators, go to parties. I also dreamed—why, I don't know—of wearing braces. Meanwhile, my somewhat lowbrow pals read *Podium* in secret, and I was scornful of them: I myself subscribed to *Astrapi*. What annoyed me, on the other hand, was that I wasn't allowed to watch television, even though I was madly in love with Albator; I dreamed that a huge man with a scarred face would carry me off to the planet Vega. Kids will be kids. And then, I read all the books that came my way. *Arrache-Coeur, Justine ou les malheurs de la vertu, Les Liaisons dangereuses* . . . I didn't understand all of it, in fact I didn't understand much. But I was making progress. And anyway, it kept me busy.

At night, on top of my little bunk bed, I had private conversations with God. I called him "Doudou." I asked great favors of him: to help me get a ninety in recitation or persuade Julien Balaski—eleven years old, gray-green eyes, and wide

Zouave pants—to sit next to me in music and drawing. Most of the time, God was merciful and generous. "Thank you, Doudou; you're a cool God." On the other hand, he never agreed to change my name to Caroline or keep papa from going off on trips so often. I don't hold it against him. All in all God did his best.

I can't say I had an unhappy childhood. I lived with papa in a large apartment he had rented because of me, opposite the Luxembourg Gardens, with temporary stepmothers who had neither the time nor the desire to become attached. Anyway, that seemed quite natural to me. Why in the world would they have loved me, Louise, shy and skinny little creature that I was? In fact, the main idea was not to draw attention to myself. Papa was often abroad. He was a fairly well-known conductor, apparently a highly gifted musician, and he didn't have a spare moment, yet he still managed to be very involved with me from a distance and do a good job of it. At school, the teacher had asked me to explain to the class what my papa did for a living. I had answered, seriously, that it was very difficult, that it involved waving his arms around a lot and leading everyone with a stick. I was four years old. Even now, I'm not convinced my answer was so absurd.

However that may be, when papa wasn't there, it was best to be as discreet as possible. Above all not to bother anyone. Move quietly, whisper, be very well behaved. No, no, I don't need anything. Yes, yes, everything's fine, I'm happy. Thank you for smiling at me, thank you for talking to me, excuse me for having a cold, excuse me thank you excuse me thank you excuse me.

But when he came home, his suitcases loaded with presents, life was a celebration. He would take me to the Louvre, to the movies, to his rehearsals. I would sit blissfully in a corner, my mind empty, feeling good. An hour of unmitigated happiness.

In order to work better, between tours, he had taken over the maid's room on the sixth floor. Every day at eleven-thirty, when I came home for lunch, I would go up there to give him a kiss, quick quick the six stories, my cheeks flaming, a stitch in my side, he would recognize my awkward little steps on the stair and always open the door just when I was about to ring. I would stay there on the landing, my index finger raised, surprised that the door had opened by magic. We would laugh and laugh. He would take me in his arms, lift me above his head, and turn around and around. I would scream with laughter, life was beautiful, and it was so good to have a papa all to myself. He told me I was pretty and that I had grown even taller overnight. I would get mad, I would say no, you're the one who's handsome, and I'm not tall, anyway I don't ever want to be tall because it would make me dizzy.

I would ask him how his work was going, and he would always answer: "Well now, you be the judge." He would sing from his score. He was something of a genius, but he sang completely out of tune. I would keep a straight face for a few minutes that lasted an eternity, and then a burst of laughter would deliver us. I suspect that he sang badly on purpose just to hear me laugh. And then we would talk and talk, I had gotten ten out of ten in dictation, I had won two marbles from Aurélie, I had seen a terrific new toy in the store downstairs, I wanted another jump rope, a kite, a red ball. We would tell each other a thousand things, all sorts of things, I forget, it wasn't important, we were the only ones in the whole world and it would be that way forever.

But unfortunately, he always had to leave again. Why? He didn't understand the question. He would explain to me: "When you're bigger, I'll take you with me, you'll see, but now you would be bored, all those stuffy old gentlemen, no one your age. . . . And anyway, I'll be back soon."

That wasn't altogether true, but I would try to convince myself; a papa always tells the truth. I missed him.

So, at night, I would slip noiselessly into his office, I took refuge from the world in the arms of his old cream-colored armchair and I would daydream quietly, happy to be there, so secret in the dimness. There was scarcely a line of light under the thick, dark velvet curtain. I felt good, I listened to the silence. A smell of cinnamon hung in the air. Sometimes I would wrap myself in one of his large black pullovers and wait for the night to pass, until I was overcome by exhaustion.

One night, when papa had been in New York for two or three weeks, I crawled into that splendid armchair of his, missing him more than ever, impatient for him to come home. There I was in his office, surrounded by books and scores, plunged in my childish thoughts, gradually yielding to the numbness of sleep, when abruptly the answering machine jolted into action and began making an awful racket: turning backward, turning forward, pausing, playing back. I realized that the zealous machine, blinking and rumbling, was only obeying papa's instructions from thousands of kilometers away. I pounced on the machine: Hello, hello papa? Papa, can you hear me? Papa? Papa, it's me! No use. Papa couldn't hear me. It wasn't so simple. He was out there, too far away, busy listening from a distance to some arrogant guys who were sure of their power and the urgency of their messages, sure that papa would call them back. They were taking their time, telling their life stories.

"Hello, Aurélien, this is Claude. A real success, the other night." *Beep beep.* "Hello dear, what's this all about? Did you read *Libe* this morning?" *Beep beep beep.* "Hello? This is the plumber. . . ." *Beep beep.* "Hello—hey pal! It's Jacques! Call me back at Denise's!" *Beep beep beep.* "Hello, this is Eléonore. We sat next to each other at L's. I didn't dare talk to you. . . ." *Beep.*

I kept my eyes fastened on the machine. It had fallen silent again. My heart was hurting me, it thumped so hard in my chest. I was alone in the world, at two o'clock in the morning, a lump in my throat, crying quietly in the dark.

10

One last memory before mama arrives. This one is important, I think. I was little, six or seven . . .

"Would mademoiselle care to order something more?"

"Excuse me?"

"Would you like some dessert?"

"No, thank you."

"Some coffee?"

"Yes. Uh, no, some tea. No, some hot chocolate. Or, yes, a tea."

"Better make up your mind!"

"Okay, coffee, please. A tall one."

"Tall and handsome?"

Silence.

"That was supposed to be a joke. Tall coffee? Tall and handsome? Right. One coffee, one! That's a change from strawberry milk, anyway."

Where was I? Yes. So when I was little, six or seven, I noticed something: What mama loved more than anything else—was it mischievousness? thoughtlessness? defiance?—was to steal little things from stores. A lavender net pullover, some Egyptian fans, two shoes for the left foot. Just making the minimum wage, in other words. At least that was what she said.

"He that will steal an egg will steal an ox"—I knew the expression. But I wasn't worried. There weren't many oxen in the shops that mama patronized. And anyway, except for our cats she didn't like animals. So I let her do it, feeling a mixture of admiration and fear as though I were on a roller coaster: terrified, but sure, deep down, that we weren't in any danger.

This could have gone on for a long time. But one evening, returning to the house in the rue Cassette, I found her in front of the building flanked by two policemen. All she said to me, in a strangely distorted voice, was:

"Don't worry, pet, I left instructions for you on my bed."

She repeated "instructions on my bed," bolstering

her words with a weak smile—the smile of a mama who was trying to be reassuring and even a little authoritative. Poor mama.

Around her wrists, bracelets of white metal, with a clasp. I was, as I said, almost seven. But I had never seen bracelets like that, nor policemen pushing someone's mama into a blue van.

Luckily, papa was there and took care of me while mama was away.

At the time he didn't have a very fixed address. It was before the period of the "temporary stepmothers" and one lover followed another with metronome-like regularity. We moved several times in a month, or even in a week. Pretty ladies, sometimes rather vacuous, would fix up a room for me in their apartment. When they annoyed me too much, or wanted me to call them mama, or when we were too far from the Luxembourg, or not close enough to school, papa would get angry, he would take me under his arm along with his scores and his blue jeans, and before you knew it he would be moving in with another woman.

For a while, he tried to make me believe that those policemen had come to take her on vacation, or to work at Disney World, or to be photographed in some far-off country. Even now, I suspect that he tried—in vain—to pull some strings with the chief warden of the Santé prison to let her out on certain Saturdays, as though she were returning from a trip and rushing over to see me.

Unfortunately, mama always said that papa was too much of a liar and she didn't like to lie. "I don't agree, Aurélien. No, no, I don't agree. Louise has a right to know. What's this bourgeois prejudice? Since when does a mother not have the right to go to prison if she chooses?"

Okay! The power of dishonesty. When mama "didn't agree," she always won her case. And that was how it happened that for four months I went to see her in prison every week.

The first few times, it was almost entertaining.

I would bring her some strawberry Yoplait, a poem, an electronic chess set. But she didn't need anything: She had fallen in with an odd assortment of women—their skin was pebbly, as though they constantly had gooseflesh—and she had taken up oil painting, and she never forgot her stomach exercises. She pretended to find the situation comical and rather enriching. "Anyway," she said, "I was sick of parading and posing for photos. At least this is a new life."

I became used to talking to her in rooms with dirty gray walls, seeing her awkwardly rigged out in a hideous uniform and sneakers, her hair pinned up severely, without makeup. She was not unattractive.

We would stay together for only half an hour. That isn't much time—half an hour—for seeing one's mama. She was the one who seemed in a hurry to leave. I would watch her walk away, her head high, proud, a queen in the wan light.

Little by little, she began to change. That was after the trial. I never really knew, but there must have been a trial, and it must have gone badly. I recall papa worrying, avoiding my questions, avoiding the questions his friends asked in front of me. And I recall her, sobered: She had a stiffer way of holding herself, a mechanical smile, a gaze that was more distant, already "after," a gaze that seemed to glide over you.

She also began to complain. Nicely, at first, mildly: "I'd like to see the sky." Or: "I'd love a long bubblebath." Or, again: "I've forgotten the taste of champagne." After which, she would say nothing and look off into the distance. I did my best to cheer her up. Well, cheer her up is saying too much. Because she no longer really smiled. She smiled without smiling, as though she didn't know how to anymore. I realized later that she no longer *dared* to. One of her teeth had broken. Was it the food? Did someone hit her? Was it the delayed effects of the drugs? A combination of all those things?

Nothing could affect me anymore. But she still wanted to spare me.

Her friends forgot to visit her, or didn't have time anymore, or didn't dare. It was so strange, after all, to go from the cover of a woman's magazine to the crime page. So they didn't know what to say, how to react. During the first few days, they relished the originality of the situation—"Yes, yes, my dear—Alice . . . the same Alice . . . a ridiculous business involving some shoplifting . . . the most idiotic incident of the season . . ." But after that, they prudently chose to keep their distance. Only a handful of paparazzi with nothing better to do continued to park themselves in the vicinity when the opportunity presented itself. What were they hoping for? Like me, no doubt, they were hoping to see her come out. . . .

During this time, mama grew weaker and began, I think, to realize the extent of the catastrophe. Thinner, circles around her eyes, her pretty skin all faded, she would still sit up straight when I came to see her, her eyelids lowered, absorbed in examining her nails or a crack in the floorboards. As for me, I moved about, made windmills with my arms as I talked. I smiled in what was supposed to be a reassuring way. But my voice seemed to take a long time reaching her. She would answer to one side, a little out of sync, numb on her chair: "yes, no." A talking doll: "I'd-like-to-I'm-thirsty-what-a-pretty-drawing." I looked for things to say. I talked to her about my friend Isabelle, or my latest grade in French; I invented the news that papa had given me a pony, or that he had changed women again, this one was very kind, or very nasty, or one day kind one day nasty, when I didn't know what else to tell. The half hour lasted for years. I was quite sure she wasn't really there, but I remained calm, dignified, I batted my eyelashes, I tried to laugh, I imagined we were in an elegant tea room somewhere.

Sometimes a phrase, a word reached her. She

would catch it on the wing. And a pale smile would light up her face. For an instant, she was there, she was listening to me. But it didn't last. Then I would compose my face to look serene, grown-up, what I had seen in movies when the actress was going to have an in-cell visit with a man condemned to death. On my way home, I would let go and cry in the street, and I would walk my sadness around all day, from the movies to the playground, from snacks with my girlfriends to dance class. I didn't say anything to my friends. The shame of understanding everything, and the shame of being ashamed. . . .

Once, I remember, I looked at her from the corner of my eye. She had gotten permission to wear makeup, which was unusual. But her face looked even more ravaged. I had actually said to myself, when I came in: "She looks like a little old woman." I gazed at her, in the poorly lighted room—her nose was running, tears rolled down her cheeks, a little powder clumsily applied had formed lumps on her high cheekbones—and I thought: "She's nothing like mama anymore." I had never seen that woman before.

Another time, she was suddenly overcome. She turned to me and moved to hug me. I recoiled. We should have tried to laugh, to see the humor of it. Neither of us thought of that. She looked bewildered, like someone who had just woken up.

Another time, I became impatient: "You're not the way you used to be! Why? Do something! Read! Work! Draw!" I stopped to think, caught my breath.

When I was very small, a friend of papa's liked to challenge me to "dare" to look him "straight in the eye," and I used to answer, from my height of seventy-five centimeters, "Yeth, I dare." In the same way now, I said to her, benevolently: "Be brave."

She smiled. In her smile there was nothing. Except, maybe, a touch of pity.

I told myself I should have helped her, done more. But I couldn't see how. So, I adopted a light tone, a lady's tone, I imagined, and said casually: "Right, ciao, see you next week." Just to say something. And, after, to cry in peace.

One day she came back home, to the house where we lived in the rue Cassette, where papa had brought me.

I never knew exactly what had happened, nor what she was guilty of. Maybe she'll tell me some day. Or right now. Yes, that would be a good subject to talk about right now, when she comes: "Tell me, mama, you remember those two policemen? And prison—was that very bad?"

Actually, no. She won't answer me. She'll give me her offended look. And she'll say: "What are you talking about, pet? Policemen? I don't believe . . ."

Because she's not cured, unfortunately. She still doesn't see things the way they are, and she still steals, though warily, and with calculation. What was only a game has become a form of revenge.

11

It was during this period that papa became seriously worried and wanted me to come live with him in rue Guynemer. This was also when I noticed all the pills mama feasted on.

She always had some with her, in her purse, loose, and she swallowed them without looking at them, like M&Ms. If you asked her what they were for, her answers were edifying: for sleeping, for waking up, for losing weight, for getting a tan, for anxiety, for hypertension, for spasms, for vertigo. Or for paresthesia, medullary aplasia, Waldenstrom's disease.

In other words: Mind your own business. Her lovers, male and female, her pharmaceuticals, her petty delinquency—these belonged to her dark side, the side of her that was kept hidden. No one had a right to see this, no one had a right to know about it. When my questions became more insistent, she would offer me her magazine smile. And she would say, very fast: "Don't worry, my kitten." Okay, okay, I wouldn't worry.

And yet I clearly felt that if I wanted to understand, if this business was going to be cleared up, if I was going to help her, maybe save her, I would have to look for the answer there, among those medicines.

So, one day, I have a sudden inspiration. I put all the tablets—pop—in my pocket. Now we'll see. I'll get them to tell me their secret in the end.

I lock myself in my room with my booty. I must be quick, not think too much. The pills dance in my pocket, I caress them, I heft them, I slip them between my fingers.

I put them on the table. I form a heart with them. I'm waiting for—what? For them to speak to me? Leap in my face like jumping beans? They certainly seem inoffensive, these little pills that do mama so much harm. Was that the abyss between us, maybe? I screw up my eyes. I imagine they're breath mints, Tic-Tacs, Haribo candies. I take a deep breath, get ready, and swallow them all at once. I stay very still. I wait. And—amazement—nothing happens.

Disappointed, or maybe relieved—maybe they were only vitamins—I go roaming around the apartment, make myself a slice of bread and butter with Nutella, put a record on the old record player, rummage around in the jewelry drawer. I try a lipstick, some sparkling powder, put on a false eyelash, just one because I think it's more chic. And then I feel an odd fatigue numbing my fingertips, then my legs, and finally I lie down on mama's bed. The record is playing: "The gates of the prison will sooooon be locked. . . ."

I look around. The wall opposite has a funny round window in it like a porthole. To the right, there's a wall papered with posters including the face of a certain *Pierrot le fou,* the face of a handsome bearded man in a beret whom mama calls "Che," a Chinese picture, an ad for Dim stockings, book covers and a drawing by me. On the other side, as a mirror, a sheet of curling aluminum foil. The carpet? Green. Milky green, or billiard green. I hate that color, mama does too, but Sophia, mama's ex, chose it, and they argued a lot. Above the bed, black-and-white photos, heaps of photos of her before, outrageously beautiful, photos of papa, her, me, crowding against one another, overlapping, an army of photos looking at me, and they don't seem pleased, they're not at all pleased. On the floor, the cat's basket overflows with unpaid tickets. There are records in piles, and books put down haphazardly, waiting for an unlikely bookcase. Farther away, garlands of bracelets, ostrich boas, a carnival mask, cushions, powder, her "pigsty." Next to me, near the bed, a cloth mannequin wearing a fringed Mexican vest. Appalling, that vest. I say a few words to the mannequin about it: "Hey, you, beanpole, your vest is dismally ugly." Not very chatty, that Aztec scarecrow. Under the night table, a bag of potato chips with a drawing on it of a young blonde woman holding. . . . My first descent into the abyss.

I feel sick to my stomach, all of a sudden. And cold. I wrap myself in the bedspread. "Like a shroud," I say to myself soberly. I had learned the word just that morning, in school.

Had I done something stupid? The walls around me begin to squeeze together, the mannequin comes closer. In a strange, childish voice, a voice like mine, it tells me mama will be home soon and I'll get a scolding.

Why is that thing getting involved? I would really like to answer it, I have some idea of putting it in its place. But I notice that I can't speak anymore. Rays of sunlight dance on the carpet. I'm having trouble breathing. The air in the room has become thick, clammy. I'm not afraid. I know I'm toppling over, but the direction I'm falling in is toward mama, toward a place where I haven't ever been able to follow her before, and soon I'll be near her, in just a minute, maybe even a second, at last I'll understand,

I'll find her again and understand. I so much want to know!

The room is full of mist, now. It's hot. It was cold, and suddenly it's the opposite, it's very hot. My head begins to swim: weird. The furniture is spinning too, but in the other direction: not so weird. Papa, in one of the photos, is shouting something I don't understand, he's shaking his head, no, no, he's opening his eyes wide, he seems frantic; I hold out my arms toward him, but something snatches me up, a frightful buzzing covers the sound of his voice, I struggle, I want to come back, I want to come back, I'm being pulled down, into the mud, I don't know how to swim, I'm going to drown, don't let me, help, I grab onto the bars of the bed, my heels beat furiously, I turn my head to the right, to the left, it's no use, I keep falling farther down, into a viscous darkness, into that chasm where, I know it now, mama falls every night, mama, wait for me, I'm coming, I coming to you, we'll be together forever. . . . I let myself sink, helpless, already defeated. I see mama down at the very bottom, she's gray, she's ugly, her complexion ruined, her face all wrong—her face made of plaster, the face of unhappiness—as in my nightmare about Snow White's stepmother.

The record continues to go around and around: "The gates of the prison will sooon be locked again, and there I'll end my liiiife, like so many other men. . . ."

❀ ❀ ❀

Mama will find me a few hours later, lifeless on her bed. Cochin Hospital, stomach pump, tears, fear, disgust, medicine locked away in a secret drawer. I'm skipping the details. Papa never knew. I must say I wasn't too proud of that adventure; mama felt even worse about it.

12

"Your coffee, mademoiselle."
"Thank you. Do you have any sugar?"
"Yes."
"Can I have some?"
"Yes."
"Why are you looking at me that way?"
"Because I have something for you."
"For me?"
"Yes, a message."

"What do you mean? Did my mother call?"

The waiter hands me a wrinkled scrap of paper napkin.

"No, he's over there, near the bar—red scarf, round glasses."

Damn! It's Dujardin. My Latin examiner at the orals. How long am I going to be stuck with him? Let's see. . . . Oh really! What a nerve! He not only sends me a love letter but writes it in Latin. If he thinks I have nothing better to do than decipher his smutty jokes. . . .

"He wants an answer."

I give the papyrus back to him.

"Tell the gentleman that it's too late for the makeup oral and anyway I don't carry my textbooks around with me when I go out."

Exit Dujardin.

But meanwhile, false alarm: mama is really going too far.

I remember the night I actually thought I was going to be angry forever. I thought I would slap her.

I'm thirteen. She has become tired of women. Or else she has realized that in fact she never liked them. Seduced by Sophia, yes. Or by feminism. Or it was simple provocation. But to make a regular thing of it—that wasn't for her.

Anyway, by now she's living in the rue Monge with a strange guy—stocky, Bourbon profile, a lisp—who works for an import-export company: thrilling.

The guy has a daughter my age, Laetitia. And now the troubles begin.

As blonde as I am dark, as sharp-tongued as I am shy, she has also stolen mama's gestures, mimicries, intonations, so that people often think she's the daughter instead of me.

What's more, she never misses a chance to let me know it. The same way of wrinkling her nose, the same fresh voice, rippling laughter . . . and the character of a pig.

Mama tries to persuade me that this girl Laetitia doesn't matter, that she's insipid, uninteresting. All the same: I really feel there is something between them—a sort of secret complicity that excludes me.

Here's what happened. We're watching television, the three of us, in the living room. Laetitia and I sitting on the floor, Laetitia in a yoga position—what a fake! Mama is smoking not far away. From time to time, they tell each other scraps of stories that I don't understand. "Private joke," Laetitia remarks to me in English.

I glare at her. She isn't offended but continues confidently: "Alice, remember the face Charles made?" More laughter. I'm humiliated. I want to make them shut up: "Quiet. I'm trying to hear the movie!" Laetitia tells me sweetly that if I'm unhappy there's another television at the corner cafe. Mama, who senses that the atmosphere is turning sour, finds nothing better to do than send me to the kitchen to get some fruit for everyone. I obey, impotent and furious.

From the kitchen, I hear the echo of their jokes, which continue. I come back, on tiptoe, as though to catch them in flagrante delicto. Halt on the threshold of the room: their shadows dancing on the floor. I hear mama whisper: "Yes, you carry a tune better than Louise." Shock. Stupefaction. I tell myself I didn't hear right, that it was an acoustical mistake. Mama wouldn't betray me like that. I'm her little girl. I'm the one she loves.

But it goes on: more outbursts of laughter, murmurs, intolerable connivance. I loom up then, my fist on my hip, plate of fruit in the other hand, determined to make them apologize. But the spectacle, from up close, goes beyond anything I could have imagined: Laetitia has laid her head on mama's knees, and mama is stroking her hair.

The fruit falls from my arms. They turn toward me at the same time. And since I must look absolutely idiotic, they burst out laughing. I remark: "Delighted to give you something more to laugh at." I'm not sure they even hear me. I don't exist anymore. Laetitia tips her head back and hangs from mama's neck. She laughs again. Her laughter is throaty, hateful, and this time there's a note of triumph in it.

I'm still on the threshold of the room, I feel pitiful, embarrassed by myself. But I won't relent. One last time, I rest my eyes on them. One last time, I inject into this all my little scorn, all my poor anger.

It's no use! Laetitia puts up with my gaze perfectly well. Will mama push her away, say something, take me in her arms? Nothing happens. Dizzying silence. I remember that she's wearing enormous pop-art glasses with orange lenses and incrusted forget-me-nots. An abomination, those glasses. But Laetitia has the ultimate audacity to remove them from her, try them on, and say with a smirk that she certainly intends to keep them on her nose. This is too much. Mama herself seems disconcerted. She says: "My kitten, my little kitten" and rests her bright eyes on me. She's hoping to pacify me. She doesn't pacify me at all. We're worlds apart at that moment.

Anguish wins out. I feel as though I'm going to cry. And out of shame I take off. Go out. Run. I don't know where I'm going. I cross in the middle of the block on purpose. If something happens to me, it will be your fault, both of you, nasties! A car brakes just in front of me. The driver, his index finger against his temple, says: "Something wrong with your brain?" Yes, something is wrong. I feel alone in the world, betrayed, nonexistent. I hate that girl. I want her to go away. I even liked it better when mama was with Sophia.

Rue de Cardinal-Lemoine, Panthéon, Saint-Michel, rue des Ecoles: My sadness, fortunately, wears off on the way back, and when I return to the rue Monge, almost nothing is left of it. My first flight from home has lasted an hour. Mama is waiting for me in front of the building. Worried? Yes, definitely worried. She says: "Forgive me." Of course

I forgive her. What is more—unhoped-for happiness—the whole evening she treats me like a convalescent. Kisses, sweet talk, promises. And also the horrible Laetitia is confined to her room until morning. So some good came of those misadventures, in the end.

Another scene, on a day long before the import-export gentleman, father of Miss Horrible. It was a very upsetting incident. I still hesitate to remember it. But okay. Today. . . . Too bad for her. All Alice has to do is get here, after all.

We're still living in the rue Cassette, in that little apartment full of junk that she shares with Sophia. I'm hardly more than five years old. I have something urgent to ask mama. (Where is my doll?) I hear splashes from the direction of the bathroom. I stick my head in the opening of the door and stay there, disconcerted: The two of them are in the bathtub. They seem to be sleeping.

Usually mama is very active in her bath. She telephones, drinks tea, sings an old Plish tune or a hit by the Stones. Now she is lying between Sophia's legs. Her head is resting on the edge of the bathtub. Her breathing is punctuated by long sighs. Odd—they have lit candles and set them on the rim of the basin, so that her face is bathed in shadow.

They haven't seen me. I'm used to that. So, I wait. I don't know what for, but I wait. And now, after a minute or two, Sophia, her eyes still closed but sitting up, begins caressing mama's shoulder with her strangler's hands. She kisses her mouth, her neck, lingers over the bend of her arm, kisses her again: They no longer seem to be sleeping at all, not at all. Sophia senses my presence, turns toward me. Not in the least surprised, no. Nor embarrassed. She looks at me with . . . greed and says, her mouth pursed: "Louise, come here, come get in the bath with us, sweetie." Her pupils shine like little round pieces of mica. I'm not her sweetie. She tries to wheedle. I find her disgusting. That swarthy complexion, those thick features, that cunning look. And that depraved smile. I don't know why, exactly, but I go off crying.

Sophia. It's funny, but I don't think I've ever remembered Sophia so intensely, so precisely, as here at the Escritoire, in this place where my father and mother met twenty years ago. Do I resent her? In the end, no. Papa had left. Mama certainly had to comfort herself. And anyway, you can get used to anything. It's crazy how a little girl ends up finding the most scandalous situations normal. And also, it could have been worse. What if mama had become infatuated with a serial killer? Or with some self-important fake like that guy over there, who's eyeing me from the next table? After all, Sophia, with her cowboy behavior, her shoulders like a Czech swimmer, her hard, thick lower lip, and her shadow of a moustache, was practically a man. Okay, she was vulgar. But she cheered things up. When she was there, you'd think a cyclone was raging through the apartment.

From time to time, when I came home from school, I would find them all excited in the living room. Maybe they had decided to read their futures in a chicken's guts. I followed the operation closely, apparently ecstatic, smiling. She sent me out for a walk: "We're not doing this for fun."

Or, on another day, she had decided to organize a demonstration against Michel Sardou, or in defense of people who wore leather pants.

Or they were taking part in idiotic televised games, decked out in wigs and moustaches so that no one would recognize them. Or there were wild schemes to swindle Sophia's ex-husband, or mama's father, or the corner grocer. Or they would exchange checkbooks, call their respective banks: "Help! I've been robbed! Stop payment immediately!" and in the meantime go on shopping orgies and have caviar parties.

Though it wasn't exactly the picture of happiness, the situation was amusing. And I ended up adopting her, that large, cantankerous woman who was such fun for mama.

Cantankerous or not, she also made real efforts to win me over. She would discreetly slip me toffees and mints, give me records by Anne Sylvestre or "Special Candy" sticker albums. That was happiness. On days when the weather was good, she would take me on her shoulders and we would go galloping off through the streets of Paris. *Tackatack, tackatack, tackatack*. . . . I can still hear it.

Sometimes she would ask me to run little errands for her, for instance, to go buy her some mysterious medicines that the pharmacist would hand over to me only after turning the prescription around in all directions, disappearing into the back room, telephoning the doctor with a very suspicious look on his face. No luck! The doctor was Sophia's brother and I could clearly sense, from the aggrieved tone of the wretched man, that he'd gotten chewed out.

It's true that Sophia seemed ill. Thin, all knees and elbows, green complexion. Well, green in the morning and yellow at night. Or olive green under her eyes and around her temples, and yellow on her cheeks. So I would run buy her something to make her better, very proud that she was relying on me.

Another time, she said to me solemnly: "I'd like to give Alice a present, you have to help me." I couldn't have asked for anything more. So she sent me to the corner cafe to collect a tightly tied-up package that I was supposed to take to the Gâité metro station and give to a gentleman who would be waiting for me on the platform. All of this, of course, was to be kept very secret if I didn't want mama to suspect anything. I carried out my task zealously and happily, all too delighted to be able to help Sophia and please mama.

Sophia, satisfied with me, began again the next week. And the week after. And again the week after that. And so on and so forth for months. There were many, many presents. There were more and more, sometimes several times a day, that Sophia had made by professional craftsmen. Why did they always have to be taken to another man who was waiting on a metro station platform, or in the square in the rue des Ecoles, or next to a trash can—and who never said thank you? I thought: Naturally, these are very beautiful gifts, maybe jewels, or inlaid boxes, or dolls with lots of different outfits, and loads of people are needed, of course, to make them and deliver them to mama.

I never saw these gifts. I only knew about the packages and the highly skilled professionals who gave them to me. They lived in smoky apartments, never said a pleasant word and emitted a rancid smell, the same smell I noticed certain mornings when I went to kiss Sophia and mama before leaving for school.

But all I thought of was mama's pleasure. And so I said nothing because I didn't want to awaken any suspicions.

But one day, one of these errands kept me longer than we thought it would, and mama, who was waiting to take me to her acupuncturist, began to worry. So that when I arrived late, my cheeks pink from running, she scolded me as she never had before. It was too unfair! It was because of her that I was late! In order to give her a pretty gift! And, very sad, then sobbing, I threw the little bag down on the floor: "Here, meanie, here's your nasty present!"

There was a funny beige-colored flour in the bag. Mama stood there for a moment disconcerted. The present must not have pleased her very much, because she was upset about it for several days. They also spent a good part of the night laying into each other, to judge from the state of the apartment the next morning.

Mama doesn't like people to make fun of her. Deciding I needed a vacation, she rented a camper and we left for the seashore, in Brittany. That's the way mama is.

And what about Sophia? She didn't go with us, for once. And after papa took me back, some time later, I never saw her again. I didn't miss her. Children are so ungrateful. . . .

I only know that she had a daughter and that she named her Louise. Apparently she would say, "little Louise" and "big Louise."

I also know that she saw mama less, then not at all, and that she went off to live in Australia, then Bangkok, then Kuala Lumpur.

She was in a motorcycle accident. Her leg had to be amputated. She tried to open a French bookstore in Bali that carried a mixture of porno comics and great literature. Last I heard, she was serving time in prison, over there, at the other end of the world, for possession of beige-colored flour and little gifts.

13

"So, has your sweetheart forgotten you?"

"Excuse me?"

"Hey, you know, I could tell you what I think of that. . . . But we have to settle up, here. I'm through for the day."

"How much do I owe you?"

"Well, let's see . . . one strawberry milk; one small coffee; one tall coffee; one decaf; a vegetable tart. I forgot the additional pickles. I won't charge you for that, you're so cute with your worried little face. . . ."

What?

"If I were you, I'd forget the guy. Standing you up like this—nice little thing like you!"

Worried little face, worried little face. . . . You should take a good look at yourself, with your dented features, your cauliflower nose. . . .

But actually, he's right: I've been shut up in this cafe too long. What time is it? Four-thirty! I ought to go and get some air. I can't stand mulling over these memories anymore. They weigh me down, they oppress me, you never come to the end of them, they never leave you in peace.

Yes, but what if she comes in the meantime? No, impossible. Besides, I'm not going far. That way, I'll see her if she comes. And also, I know her: She'll sit down, order her beer, which she won't drink, and meet some old buddy from her childhood. That's the way it is with mama—when she meets someone, it's always a childhood friend, and she has enough of them to spend hours finding them again. So, not to worry. I can go stroll around and stretch my legs a little.

Another solution: call a girlfriend. Clotilde, Nathalie, Pauline? "Hi, I have an hour to kill, I'm depressed, want to come be bored with me?" That way, without moving, I could change my mood. Oh, forget it! I'm sick of being stuck here. For six hours—six hours!—I've been waiting for her here, like a dope. It's getting crazy. And it would be the last straw if she chose this exact moment to show up. So I'm going for a walk. Tralala.

I'll go over to the bookstore. After all, I'm supposed to be a student, I guess. But actually, at the moment, I'm nothing. I was supposed to prepare for the poli sci entrance exam. But it turned out to be the very same day as my birthday. Coincidences do happen.

Before that, I had embarked on a career in music, like papa. But (I've noticed there's always a "but" coming along to interfere with fate) one day, by chance, in the living room bookcase, I discovered a book about psychoanalysis and stumbled on the theme of the Oedipus complex. "Kill the father." So, just like that, the child is supposed to "kill" its father? Out of the question. And I decided overnight to stop my piano lessons, voice lessons, dance lessons, and devote myself to physics and chemistry.

I was twelve years old. My music teacher, an excitable old homosexual, cried sacrilege. Papa couldn't really understand it either. "What an idea, my dear, you're so gifted." As for mama, she couldn't see what was happening, and couldn't care less anyway. Result: I never touched the piano again in my life. Oh, so you're supposed to "murder" your father? Well, I'd show them! I would spend my days resolving cubic equations.

The result, six years later, is: a bachelor's in science; no-show on the day of the entrance exam for poli sci; papa who wants to send me to Assas—talk about a present! Penal law, constitutional law, international law, healthy atmosphere, short hair, baseball bats and relaxed little fascists. And then, and then, this frightful doubt: What if I was wrong, after all? What if I had killed him by disappointing him? He was hoping for so much from me.

Starting from when I was born, he took me—but I was told this too late—to all the famous places that were supposed to accept me some day. We walked past the Lycée Henri IV and the Lycée Louis le Grand, the Ecole Normale de Musique in the rue Cardinet, and even the Panthéon, because it was on the way. He also introduced me, apparently, to the Louvre, the Opéra de Paris, and the Elysée. I was supposed to strive for the best. With the same question always tormenting me: How to be worthy of him, and not play Oedipus to his Laius?

Okay. Never mind all that. Here I am, in the basement of the bookstore, trying to choose an exciting novel. Let's see. *Aurélien,* because that's papa's name. *Gilles,* because there's a character in it who's like mama. Apollinaire's *Seated Woman.* That biography of Romain Gary. A Truman Capote—no, I've read them all. The Sybille Lacan, because in the "kill your father" category apparently no one does it better. *Eighteenth Year* by Jean Prévost, that's appropriate. Oh no! I've got it! Süskind. *Perfume.* That's exactly what I need. Just the sort of book she would love.

"Excuse me, monsieur. . . ."

"Actually, my name is Sandra."

"Oh, I'm really really sorry! I'm looking for a book. . . ."

"You're not the only one."

"Maybe you could help me?"

"I'm not paid to do that. Ask someone who works here."

"Hi."

"Hi."

"Could you help me?"

"What is it?"

"Do you know anything about *Perfume?*"

"Well, I bathe! What do you take me for?"

"I was talking about Patrick Süskind. . . ."

"Patrick who?"

"Süskind."

"Never heard of him."

"Maybe it's on the shelf. . . ."

"First of all: I bathe. Second: I'm not a salesperson."

Okay. So much for *Perfume.* This basement is barbaric. And anyway, it's much too hot. Quick, get out. Buy *Le Nouvel Obs,* that'll be enough. And then find some pretty flowers. Roses? Violets? Lilies? Or something exotic instead. I don't know much about it, but I know she'll like that. Somewhere in Albert Cohen I read: "They're sensitive to those plants."

Return to the Escritoire. With a cactus. Definitely a mistake, this cactus. What possessed me to choose it? I should have stuck to the lilies. I always allow myself to be had. A florist who's too friendly, rather ugly, I feel a little sorry for her. . . . And here I am with an old shopworn cactus.

I was gone barely a half hour and already the people are different. Same laughter, same hubbub, same cheeks swollen with chewing, all in all the same theater. But the actors are different. And mama still isn't here. It's a quarter to six. Is she ever going to show up?

Examination of conscience. Did I do something wrong? Is she cross with me? But about what?

Putting a rubber snake in her bed? That wasn't very elegant, I admit. But I wasn't even six yet. And anyway, she deserved it. The Dior dress I borrowed from her two years ago and wore to school? To that I plead guilty, even if it was quite fair. But I paid rather heavily for it, no point in going back to that. Tortured by remorse? I can't even sleep at night anymore. Childish? Oh yes! Insolent? That would be common courtesy. I'm wrong to laugh about it? Great.

And what if there is . . . a deeper misunderstanding? An old rift, which these months of silence have only widened? I don't know. I'll have to wait. Let's just say that will be the first question I ask her.

14

A doubt, all of a sudden. How long did I stay away, including the bookstore without *Perfume* and the cactus saleswoman? Thirty minutes! Forty, maybe! And what if she came? And went away again? No. She would have sat down. She would have ordered something to drink. The childhood friend, blah blah blah. And also the place would have preserved a trace of her. There would be a marital squabble at the table on the right. That girl over there would be making a face, rigid with jealousy. Her fiancé, who's greedily drinking his cocoa, would try to placate her, but his eyes would still be sparkling. Everyone here would be saying to each other, like in that song by Starmania: "Who was that creature? Look at that woman! What style!"

Let's see. Quick check. What's that guy on my right talking about, and on my left, and in the background?

"Hue versus Jospin, you understand the practical aspect, right. . . . I tell you that dope is a real bitch. . . . American flicks—that's where it's at. . . . I'll tell you, the new security system really bugs me. . . . Hey, what would we do without that security system they've got now. . . . I think it's serious between Barbra Streisand and Prince Charles. . . . My parents say when they were kids, in '68. . . . Check out Diana's new plastered-down look. . . . Claudia Schiffer—not so great, they say she has false teeth. . . ."

This is the Sorbonne. These are the students I used to dream about all the time. And not a word about mama. The bastards! No, it's really okay. It's because she didn't come.

"Excuse me, waiter?"

"Yeah?"

"I left for a few minutes and. . . ."

" 'Management is not responsible for the loss or theft of objects deposited on the ground without being watched.' "

"The object, as it happens, is my mother. She didn't by any chance come in while I was gone?"

"Hey, do I look like a lost and found department?"

Charming guy, that waiter.

Second waiter.

"Excuse me, waiter?"

"What would you like?"

"Another coffee, please. And I also have a question."

"One espresso, one!"

"My question is. . . ."

Too late. Won't anyone help me?

"Is there some problem, mademoiselle?"

Who's this guy with the beard? He certainly isn't a waiter. "You seem to be rather upset."

What's it to him? Oh, well, after all. . . .

"I was supposed to meet someone but I'm afraid she may have gotten here before me, well actually she's the one who was late but I went out for five minutes, well actually a little longer than that and she must have thought I hadn't waited for her but I'm still here and I'm waiting for her though maybe it's pointless."

"I see."

"The fact is I'm looking for my mother."

"And what does your mother look like?"

"Like someone out of a dream. Outrageous, fantastic, she always orders a beer and never drinks it, her name is Alice but she doesn't like it, she loves *Pierrot le fou* and Françoise Hardy."

"Hmm . . . hmm. You wouldn't have a photo?"

"Five feet eight. A hundred and twenty-one pounds. Thirty-eight years old. Redhead. Long hair. Large eyes, green. Eyebrows à la Greta Garbo. A beauty mark near her lip. Smokes with her left hand. Shalimar by Guerlain. Will that do?"

"A photo would still. . . ."

"A . . . yes, of course, here."

"Good. Don't be sad. Sit down and. . . ."

I'm not sad and I'm already sitting down.

"All right, stay there. I'll go find out. If anyone has seen your Madonna he'll certainly remember."

Why did I lie about her age? A matter of two years—that's absurd. She herself never does. But I've always been coy for her. When I was little, between four and seven years old, when we lived together, before papa took me back, I refused to go out if she wasn't impeccably made up—spangles on her eyelids, her mouth like a cherry—with equally fine shoes on her feet; the ones I loved the most were a pair of pumps with very high stiletto heels. The fact was, I wanted her to be the way she was in the magazines, I wanted people to recognize her and whisper when she went by. I would choose her outfits very carefully, and the color of her jewels. And I was uncompromising: "Oh, no!" I would say with a sigh which I tried to make exasperated, "you can't go out like that, your nail polish is sloppy, and you forgot your hat!"

I would send her back to her closets: "We'll leave when you're really ready!"

And she would give in to my whims. She would reappear, divine, new jacket, pretty scarf. I would inspect her, I would step back, I would tuck up a sleeve and, pint-sized though I was, I would give my verdict: "Okay, that's good."

She would bite her lip to keep from laughing. And we would go off to buy bread, arm in arm, chattering away. But I remained on my guard: close to her, on the lookout for a stray wisp of hair or a wandering shoulder strap. She would crouch down close to me in the middle of the sidewalk or the street. She would call me "my little chaperone, my tiny little three-foot-high chaperone," and, among the blaring horns, allow me to tend to every detail of her toilette.

As time went by, our relationship changed. And I would even say that in the last two or three years it has been reversed. She wants boys to like me, she lavishes a thousand pieces of advice on me about how to be seductive, and I sometimes have the feeling she would like to—how should I put it?—have me be attractive instead of her.

One memory, among others. Two years ago. She was going out with a young prima donna, a guy ten or fifteen years younger than her, a bit of a loafer, a bit of a joker, an aspiring actor in the free class at Florent and apparently a member of a partner-swapping club in the rue Princesse. It seemed funny to me and rather stupid that mama had become infatuated with this God's gift to women. And I have to confess I quite liked the boy: I found him exotic.

But she started a funny kind of game: flattering me in front of him, endlessly praising my long legs and my opulent chest, boasting about my docility or my humor. In fact, there's only one way to put it: She was trying to sell me.

In the beginning, I didn't really understand. I only blushed and asked her to stop. Then, this boy, Grégoire, began to outdo her—"Absolutely, and what skin! So delicate! And her mouth! A strawberry!"—and I began to find the interaction rather unwholesome. So I tried to keep my distance.

One Saturday, however, he was there on his motorbike in front of the school: "Come with me."

I declined, he insisted: "Alice is waiting for us at Vavin."

Alice wasn't waiting for us at all. Alice, as I learned the next day, was in Limousin. Was this a plot? She has always denied it. But the fact is that after half an hour of conversation, after numerous more or less direct advances, obscene puns and then, finally, a frankly bold move, I kicked him hard in the shin and called him—supreme insult—a stupid jerk.

"Mademoiselle . . . mademoiselle?"

"Yes?"

"Here's my report: Seven people never saw your mother, two are sure they passed her a little while ago, three begged me for her phone number and the last one asked me where she was last Wednesday between four and six in the morning, at the time of the double murder in Parc Montsouris."

"Now I'm really getting somewhere."

"If I were you, I'd go call her."

"Impossible. No way of reaching her."

"And how long have you been waiting for her?"

"A while."

"I see. And how much longer are you thinking of staying here?"

"As long as it takes."

"Right. I'm waiting for someone too. I was wondering if. . . ."

"I have a ton of work to do."

"Oh, okay. . . . What kind of work?"

" 'The Formation and Displacement of Scientific Concepts in Georges Canguilhem.' It's my master's thesis."

Poor guy, I certainly disposed of him. He was rather obliging. But after all, it's his own fault if he looks more like Danny DeVito than Daniel Day Lewis.

"Mademoiselle?"

"What now!"

"Is your name Louise H.?"

"Yes."

"There was a call for you half an hour ago, but you weren't here. It was a gentleman. Calling for your mother. He left a message."

"What message?"

"Let's not panic now."

He shouts, his hands cupped around his mouth: "Mamao! Mo-mo! What did that guy say, for the girl at three? What?"

Resuming a normal voice:

"Right, okay: 'Wait for Alice, she's going to come.' "

"That's all? The man didn't say who he was? He didn't say where he was calling from? Is everything all right? He didn't give any explanation?"

"Mamao! Mo-mo!"

"No, that's okay, never mind, thanks."

Okay. Louise, get hold of yourself. Your mother's going to come. Finally! That's wonderful! Although. . . . With her, anything is always possible. Including getting out of the cab on the way, deciding it would be more fun to take the metro, changing at Concorde instead of Chatelet, meeting some self-styled musician passing the hat in a subway car and inviting him to a salsa evening that will go on until tomorrow. Sophia always used to say: "With Alice, it's very simple—you have to expect the worst."

15

Remember that day when you thought she had abandoned you. . . .

You're not quite five years old yet. You're all at Rennes. Sophia and your mother take you to the square in the historic part, the center of town. You have a feeling it's all going to be fun, you run around like a crazy puppy, you ask for cotton candy, they even buy you a wooden hoop and stick; life is neat.

All of a sudden they spot a big girl, maybe ten years old, on a scooter: "Look, Louise, she seems friendly!"

You don't answer. You think she's ugly. You throw sand at a pigeon to show your annoyance. The gesture misfires. They think it's charming, and so does the girl.

"What's your name, honey?" asks your mother with a sprightly air.

"Jessica. What's yours?" answers the girl, tossing her hair.

"I'm Alice. That's Sophia. And the little one hiding behind me sucking her thumb—nasty habit!—is my daughter Louise."

"Hi," the girl says cautiously, with a crooked smile.

Sophia and Alice exchange looks, then Sophia takes over.

"Tell me, Jessica, would you like to earn thirty francs?"

Her tone is supposed to be full of initiative. Anyway, she's right on the mark: Big Jessica's eyes are shining like her necklace of plastic pearls. But the kid won't allow herself to be taken advantage of:

"With thirty francs, you can't even buy a Barbie doll!"

"And how much would you need for a Barbie doll?"

"At least thirty-five francs!"

"Well, listen: I'll give it to you."

What's happening to her? Has she gone crazy?

Why does she want to give a present to that show-off?

The girl, meanwhile, is in seventh heaven, gloating over the windfall. Then, a suspicion:

"And what do I have to do?"

Waiting for the answer, she turns her head away slyly and traces circles in the sand with the tip of her shoe.

"Easy—you play with Louise while we do some shopping."

"Shopping to buy my Barbie doll?"

"To buy your Barbie doll."

"Magic-Barbie-and-her-dream-hairstyle?"

"Magic-Barbie-and-her-dream-hairstyle."

"Terrif! Come on, Louise, let's play tag!"

At that moment I look up at mama, I imagine she's going to burst out laughing, cry: "Oh, what a good joke! We really fooled her!"

But no. She avoids my eyes. She smiles at the frightful little girl, goes into raptures over the girl's scooter, says they won't be long, that we must be good and not talk to strangers.

I should have yelled, jumped up and down, faked an epileptic fit. But I don't yell, I don't cry, I barely try to hide in the skirts of the two traitors. The big girl examines me, she thinks about her Barbie doll, she smiles.

Mama leans over toward me. She presses a kiss on my forehead. She doesn't see the distress in my face, she doesn't see the look in my eyes, the look of a very small girl who was counting on her to roll the hoop together and spend the afternoon laughing and singing. She says: "Be good now, pet, and above all stay with Jessica." Then Sophia takes her arm, and they walk off briskly without turning back.

I see them move away in the yellow light. I fill my eyes with it. Their long legs are like knitting needles. Now they're only a small dot. Now they're no more than a little dust. It seems to me I can still hear mama's bright laughter.

Jessica looks me up and down in silence for a moment with a smile that I imagine, today, to be at once depraved and mocking. Then she blurts at me:

"How old are you?"

"Four and a half."

"I suppose you know how babies are made?"

I lift my chin bravely:

"Yes, I know."

"Then go on, tell me."

"No, I won't tell you."

I stand my ground in front of her, my little fists squeezed tight, deep in my pockets.

"That means you don't know."

"Yes I do."

"No you don't."

"Yes I do."

"Then why don't you want to tell?"

"Because."

"Because what?"

"Because. Because."

We stay there face to face, sudden gusts of wind

lift the sand in little waves, people passing by bump into us without excusing themselves. I put my thumb in my mouth in order to seem very busy.

The big girl returns to the charge with a self-satisfied look.

"Do you know what a nuterus is?"

I don't answer, more and more I feel like crying. She goes on:

"And a numbilical cord—do you know about that?"

That's it, I sob quietly, rubbing my fists against my eyes. What does that girl want from me? Why is she pestering me?

She seems suddenly gentler. Her eyes coax me. She takes me by the shoulders.

"Here, I'll explain it to you."

The moment that follows is one of the longest in my life as a child.

Jessica, all pink and blonde, turns serious and begins describing in detail the different stages of procreation, spermatozoids, ovulation, pregnancy, the illnesses of pregnancy, the first labor pains—why doesn't she shut up! Shup up! Just shut up! She goes on worse than before, very animated, her cheeks flaming, and she describes how the baby comes out between the legs, upside down, covered with blood, how people help it with a sort of knife, with pincers, how the mommy yells, the baby yells, the doctor yells, the midwife yells, everyone yells. . . . At that, I go and vomit in a clump of budding tulips.

❀ ❀ ❀

The little girl walks over to me:

"Hey pal, what's the matter, don't you feel well, are you sick?"

Me, sick? I'm bent over, quite red, almost violet, my eyes starting from my head, shaking with spasms, my face stained with tears and vomit. Sick?

Jessica looks to the right, to the left. Phew! No one is paying any attention to us. She mounts her scooter and takes off, rolling like a marble down the winding paths.

Sophia and Alice will reappear a thousand years later jabbering like geese, delighted with what they've bought, with their afternoon. Meanwhile, I've ended up in some lookout post of the garden, crouched in a corner, a shivering, filthy little thing, staring into space. I imagine I'm poor, abandoned Candy, who's going to be taken to Mademoiselle Pony's orphanage and will never see her papa again.

Did they remember the Barbie doll?

I can't be sure anymore. But it seems to me they didn't.

16

I was nearly five, then, when I was "abandoned." Old enough to complain. Did I? Who did I complain to? However it may have been, the fact is that the following week papa took action and I was placed in the care of my first nanny, Malika. She didn't last long in the job. Even from a distance, papa eventually realized that instead of taking me to the seesaws in the Luxembourg Gardens, this attentive young lady would knock me out with a sedative and then deposit me on a couch at her lover's place.

I had better luck with the second. Her name was Aimée. We called her Madame Aimée, and for a long time I thought her name was Madamémé. This name—"Beloved"—should have been a good omen. And in fact, she was true to it: Infinitely loving and tender, she taught me to feed the sparrows, allowed me into her bed in the morning and made the best polenta.

One day, unfortunately, no doubt diagnosing a maternal deficiency concerning the matter, she decided to "take my education in hand." And so it was that I entered a church for the first time.

I was about to turn five. She explained to me: "It's very simple; you sit down, you don't suck your thumb, you watch what other people do and you do exactly the same thing."

It seemed easy: "Exactly the same thing."

And because I wanted her to be very pleased with me, I was zealous: I hid my hands behind my back, I looked straight ahead with the most reasonable air—a cinch—and then, when everyone stood up to intone a song I didn't know since I hadn't learned it at school, I thought for a moment and began singing also, very loudly, right on tune, right in time—but what I sang was *"Au clair de la lune, mon ami Pierrot . . ."*

Madamémé was not at all pleased. We left

abruptly before the end of the show. She didn't utter a word all the way home and gave up "concerning herself with my education." Papa, to whom I described the incident, explained to her that it was just as well this way, seeing that we weren't really Catholics. Madamémé was pained. Often, after that, she would look at me sadly, wag her head, stroke my hair, and sigh with a woebegone air: "Poor, poor little child. . . ."

Were the two things related? Madamémé fell ill at about that same time and left us very suddenly. The truth was she was no longer very young and her varicose veins hurt her. She never complained. She said it was the Good Lord who wanted it that way. The Good Lord? My Good Lord? The good "Doudou" who helped me get nice presents and good grades in recitation? How could he endure Madamémé's nasty varicose veins? Now there was a puzzle! I said to myself that Madamémé must be making a mistake when she said her prayers. She must be reversing words, or talking in dialect or not pronouncing clearly enough. I would certainly have told her to pay more attention, but I was afraid of annoying her. Adults are so sensitive sometimes! And God is even more so! One day she fell from a bridge where she lived, near Bordeaux, and I never saw her again.

The day I turned five, papa sent us a third nanny whose name was Marie-Ange. She had no children and she found me cute, plump and dimpled, so she adopted me right away. I remember a lady with chestnut hair pinned up in a bun, precise gestures and slate gray eyes, who would walk me to school at a vigorous pace, one-two, one-two, it was such fun, and who would let me watch television in her room until the movie was over, even when it ended late.

Life with her was good. It was fine. But Marie-Ange too had to leave. I'm going to get married, she explained to me, tears in her eyes. I found that a little strange, since you could only get married if you were twenty years old, blonde with blue eyes, and had found your Prince Charming. Marie-Ange wasn't very young anymore. She was fifty years old, maybe more, heaps of little wrinkles at the corners of her eyes, and she had shown me a photo of her sweetheart—he was very ugly, very old, with a shabby checked jacket and an odd smile; too many teeth on one side, none at all on the other. I didn't want her to leave. So I told her her husband looked like a bear. She could have taken that the wrong way. I was lucky, it made her laugh. She hugged me against her chest. Then she took up her fat, light brown valise, and I never saw her again either. Later I learned that she had found another position, with other people, with other children. But then why, why had she left us? What did those people have that was better than what we had? The two of us had been so happy. . . .

❀ ❀ ❀

Long after, I understood: She couldn't stand mama, her disorder, her lovers. She couldn't face stumbling over syringes anymore, answering the neighbors' spiteful remarks and confronting their stares when she encountered them in the local shops.

17

What's all the commotion? Oh I see, it's the big guy in the stripes over there. Why's he getting as mad as a hornet?

"Look, madame, I smoke *the* cigar I want to, *where* I want and *when* I want! But it won't bother me in the least if you choose not to smoke."

"No, monsieur," answers the little curly-headed woman at the next table, "you don't do what suits you, monsieur! We"—she looks to her audience to be witnesses—"won't tolerate your nauseating, carcinogenic fumes."

"Madame's lungs are delicate? Perhaps she'd like to go take the cure at Saint-Joie-les-Gouttes!"

The waiter intervenes:

"Hey! What's going on?"

"What's going on is that this lady with physical disabilities is bothering everyone with her lung problems."

"What a nerve!" explodes the little woman, beside herself. "This pig is stinking up the place with his cheap tobacco!"

"Actually, this part of the room is reserved for non-smoking customers," the waiter says, deciding the matter.

"That's what I said," the curly-headed woman says exultantly.

"Bravo," declares the big man in stripes as he stands up, bows and in passing blows a stream of smoke in her face.

It's funny, something like this would never happen to mama. She has always smoked wherever she wanted, even in the movies, and with such assurance that no one dares to scold her. Mama and her insolence. . . . Whereas last night at the Montparnasse UGC, some carping woman said to me "This isn't a circus, you know!" because I was making a little too much noise with my candy wrappers. Well, it wasn't church either!

❀ ❀ ❀

Anyway, it's six-thirty. Mama has never been so late. And I'm beginning to wonder if she'll ever show up. Could I have been wrong about where we were meeting? No, since she had someone call. The time? She said she was coming. Could there be some problem? Some silly thing that's delaying her? Yes, that would certainly be like her. She's capable of walking off with the musician or stopping by at a friend's place and trying to reform the world. She'll notice what time it is, take him by the hand, and say: "Come on, honey, I don't agree but we can go on arguing while we walk. I have a date with Louise, you'll see how much fun she is, you'll see we're not at all alike." That would be typical too. Anything to avoid an intimate conversation, confidences and embarrassing questions.

I remember one time: I was thirteen or fourteen, we were supposed to spend a couple of days together in the country. I was living with papa, and she was only allowed to take me every other weekend and half the vacations. So it was Saturday at noon. School was out. I was waiting for her at the Vavin in a fever of excitement, as usual. I'm so happy to see her! I have so many secrets to tell her! There are a thousand and one treasures in my overnight bag: an eighty in composition, a black-and-white collage, photos of my friend Isabelle and me at the dance class show.

But when she arrives—late, of course—she's flanked by a big bony guy with an unpleasant sneer on his face.

"This is Pierre-André."

The guy corrects her: "Call me Joe," he says in English.

Some bizarre remarks follow, delivered like a telegram: "It's hot slept too long I'm thirsty a Coke your daughter a beer too cool Raoul not too early."

I tell myself mama met him by chance, she asked him along for a drink just to be polite and he'll leave soon. Besides, he himself looks as though he's wondering what he's doing here.

As polite as mama, I ask:

"And what do you do in life, Monsieur Joe?"

"I hang around."

Nervous laugh from me. Shrug of the shoulders from mama. Then, after a long silence and trying not to look too stupid:

"Neat shirt!"

And he says, punctuating his remark by clearing his throat noisily:

"Yeah, I know, yeah."

Thrilling.

When a person doesn't say anything, I usually think he's enigmatic, wrapped in mystery, I think he has all sorts of hidden depths. But obviously this one is not thinking about *anything*. He's sitting there, flabby, motionless. He imposes his presence, his Marlboros, his abrupt gestures, his thick blue veins on his hands and his fingers, which I imagine on mama's body. Intolerable. No. That freak can't be her lover.

Meanwhile, he's there, mineral, heavy.

I should be able to take mama in my arms, kiss her on the nose, say to her: "I missed you, you smell good, let me light your cigarette, let's go." But in front of him I don't dare. I just sit there, my hands resting sedately on my knees, sipping my Coke, blowing bubbles with my straw—because it tastes better that way and mama has allowed me to ever since I was three years old.

I tell myself he'll get up soon, go play pinball, call someone, he must be getting antsy from sitting still so long. While he's away, I'll devise an escape plan: "Quick, quick," I'll say to mama, "let's say we have to take off, let's say someone's waiting for us at the other end of the city, that we're late, or even better, let's just take off without telling him, it's safer and funnier."

But no, the guy doesn't move, he's fine, he throws his head back and blows smoke rings. From time to time, he glances at Alice: Maybe he wants to see if she's impressed, maybe not. Anyway, she's off in another direction, as vague as he is, her chin on her hand, smiling into space. I've definitely seen her looking better. She's like me: She must be waiting for him to go away, she doesn't dare drive him off and thinks he'll get the idea on his own.

Okay. After all, I'm with her. We have two days of happiness in front of us. I can certainly endure Mr. Call-Me-Joe for an hour or two. So I keep myself occupied, I put mustard in the ashtray and Coke in the mustard. But the fellow still doesn't move. He entertains himself with the bits of skin around his nails and he whistles between his teeth. Mama orders something else to drink: "A glass of wine, please." The empty glasses are lining up on the table. Six already. I'm afraid mama may be getting drunk. She is rarely happy when she's been drinking. And then I'm not sure she has enough to pay the tab. I don't want to run out of here the way we sometimes do. I pass the Vavin four times a day.

And then, a miracle! Call-Me-Joe, emerging from his torpor and spitting one last crescent of fingernail on the table—really, this guy is repulsive—decides to move at last.

"Okay, girls, let's get going."

Off in the direction of Issy-les-Moulineaux, where he lives in a horrible little detached house with what he calls his "gang."

When we get there, the members of the aforementioned gang are sprawled on mattresses and sleeping bags on the bare floor. The air is filled with a dreadful smell of old goat, which doesn't seem to bother anyone. A little apart, a boy with no shirt on, his back rounded, plays a tune from the sixties on his guitar, beating time to it with his head: yeah, yeah.

Farther away, two nasty-looking creatures seem absorbed in reading a magazine under the attentive eye of a Siamese cat.

The only woman in the group, her nose bulbous and her hair in her face, is lying on the floor, her arms crossed on her chest.

Dull glances in our direction.

I risk a shy smile.

At which, Call-Me-Joe, who has unbuttoned his shirt down to the navel, declares, not without some pride:

"Girls, these are my buddies: Manu, Pat (hey old man!), Nancy (who's off in the clouds), Rapetou, Mic, Gérard and Bill."

Then:

"Guys: I've told you about Alice; the young lady next to her is Louise. Yeah, daughter of. Watch yourselves now, she's a minor."

He sits down next to the one named Pat and lights a gigantic cone for himself. I try to seem neutral, to arrange my face to look blasé, as though I'm used to this. But I must admit that with my miniskirt, my Agnes B cardigan and my neat braid, I don't really blend in with the scene.

I sit down on the floor next to Bill, who looks like a monk. And then I make the most absurd gesture imaginable: I hold out my hand to him. I can't help it. My years of good upbringing are more powerful than any sense of absurdity.

The monk blows smoke in my face. Brick red, overcome by a desire to cough, I look desperately in mama's direction. Her sharp profile, against the black background of the wall behind her. That strange way of rolling her cigarette. Her expression, that of a diligent little girl, the tip of her tongue between her teeth. Is this the dream weekend? Is this all she can think of to offer me?

I feel a furious desire to go to her, shake her, bring her back to life. Tell her: You're crazy, what are we doing with these losers, wake up, this isn't what you promised me! Didn't you tell me we were going to the country?

She lifts her eyes to me, her large green eyes pricked with gold. But she's looking at me without seeing me, already gone, staring at a point that is very distant, well beyond the leprous wall, above her lolling friends. Only her perfume, sweet and enveloping, is still like her, and reaches me. Is this still mama? My little mama that I was waiting for so impatiently just a few hours earlier? A vein is throbbing on her neck, and I recognize it.

I ought to stand up, resolute, haughty, a sarcastic smile on my lips, and leave with dignity: I despise you, all of you, I despise you. I would like to be someone else, to be stronger, prouder. But though years have passed, I'm still afraid of upsetting things, and I hardly dare move. So far from mama, so close to tears.

And then, providence! I notice the Siamese cat, who's playing on a cushion.

"Here kitty, *psst,* look at me, puss puss . . ."

The cat comes and sniffs my hand, walks around me for a few seconds, then settles on my knees, purring. Who said a dog was man's best friend?

I'm saved: Joe's friends are the sort of people who trust the instincts of animals. And now Gérard comes over to tell me a funny story; Nancy, smiling widely, offers me a beer; and even Rapetou lends me *Coke en stock* and *L'Etoile mystérieuse.*

I'm not asking for that much. Confused, I say: "Thanks, sorry, thanks a lot." I drink a mouthful of beer and begin leafing through the Tintin books. I would have accepted anything.

The weekend will pass rather quickly, in the end.

Sunday evening.

My new friends say good-bye, see you next week, what are you doing over vacation, they offer me a few joints in the meantime and make me promise to call often. I promise, crossing my fingers.

18

Hey. That young man over there, on the square, that big dark overcoat, that face—so pale it's as though the blood has drained from his face. It seems to me. . . . Could it be him? Adrien? All the time I've been waiting for him. . . . I know everything about him. Everything. We've never spoken, I've never seen him from so close up, but I really think. . . . He goes to school at

Henri IV. He's nineteen years old. Lives in a studio in the rue Bréa. Alone. Girlfriend, unfortunately. Likes Shakespeare, Molière and soccer. Also likes. . . . Hey! He's coming toward me! It's him, no doubt about it, and he's coming straight over to me! What expression should I have? If only I were able to smoke without coughing. And I look so stupid with my cactus. Cactus under the table. He's here, he's going to come into the cafe, my lipstick probably rubbed off on the coffee cup, too bad, he's pushing open the door, he sees me, he's smiling at me, he's standing in front of me, help!

"Hello, Louise. It is Louise, isn't it?"

"Yes, that's right," I say, picking up my little spoon in order to do something with my hands.

"I'm Adrien."

"Oh." (No kidding.)

"You waiting for someone?"

"No, no."

(Yes you are, idiot! Your schedule is as full as the president's! Not a second to yourself!)

"Well, I mean. . . . Yes . . . I am actually waiting for someone. . . ."

(Louise, put your spoon down before you do something else that's stupid.)

"I'm meeting someone too, but. . . . Do you mind if I sit down, since we're both waiting?"

(There, I knew it, the little spoon is completely twisted. Poof, under the table, along with the cactus.)

"Oh, you dropped something. . . ."

"I did?"

"Yes, here, look, your spoon. Hey, look at this, when you stir your coffee . . ."

"No, they gave it to me like that."

(Here we go, I'm blushing, I bet I'm blushing.)

"They gave it to you twisted, mangled like this? Well, they're kind of careless here, aren't they! Waiter!"

(Sarcastic half-smile. Could he be making fun of me?)

"No, no! It's not his fault, the poor thing, he's overwhelmed, and anyway, I don't need the spoon."

(I'm talking more and more quickly, in a rush, I'm swallowing half the words. Louise, calm down, take a deep breath. Zen.)

"Have you noticed? We keep bumping into each other and this is the first time we've spoken."

"Uh. . . ."

(The sun is in his face and his eyes are half closed. With any luck, he hasn't noticed that I'm crimson. Anyway, he's going on.)

"I heard you wanted to try poli sci?"

"Yes, but I gave up on it."

"You probably have a good reason."

(How clumsy of you! You've disappointed him terribly! Besides, you don't have to tell him your whole life story!)

"Louise, careful, don't move."

"What?"

"I said, don't move."

(He's taking hold of my wrist. He's moving his face close to mine. His peppery perfume is surrounding me, caressing me. Is he going to kiss me? Already? I encourage him with a smile.) He says:

"Make a wish, you have an eyelash on your cheek."

"A wish? . . . Done."

(My wish is: Stop blushing, stop blushing, stop blushing!)

He brushes my cheekbone with his forefinger. I turn violet with confusion. Great wish! Thanks up there, Doudou!

"You skin is as soft as a baby's."

"Is that a compliment?"

"What do you think?"

"I don't know—babies are wrinkled."

"We don't know the same babies." Then, in English: "Do you mind if I smoke?"

"Uh. . . ." In English: "Yes, no, please, please do."

Watch out, Louise, you're about to look ridiculous! It's true that the situation is becoming awfully embarrassing. Okay. Choose your weapon. Imagine him at the dentist, his mouth wide open, he's going *aaaahhh,* he has a horrible cavity in the back on the right.

"Louise, are you listening to me?"

"Excuse me?"

"I said: Are you listening to me?"

"Yes."

"I have to go."

"Okay."

Hunh! He's not that good-looking after all. Also, he's missing a button on his shirt.

"Listen, Louise, I'd like to see you again."

See me again! Mama! Listen to that! He wants to see me again! Him! The best looking boy in the world! The two of us together!

"Uh. . . . Maybe. Let me think about it."

"Right, I understand."

Well, look at that. He's the one who seems disturbed now. The blood is rushing to his face and—at last!—his prominent cheekbones are turning red. And also, for the past three minutes he's been crumbling bread on the table. How cute.

"Is that for the pigeons?"

"What?"

"The bread: Is it for the pigeons?"

"No. . . it's a bad habit."

"Look, it's no worse than twisting little spoons."

"Except that it's repulsive."

"No it's not."

The little heap of crumbs is soaked with cold coffee.

A waiter wipes off the table with a disapproving scowl. We burst out laughing.

"Are you doing anything tomorrow night?"

"I'm busy."

"What about the day after tomorrow?"

"Busy then too."

"Well, when? Tell me when would be good!"

"Tonight."

"What?"

"I said tonight, I'm free tonight."

His lips curl up in a delighted smile. He looks like a child.

"Tonight? Great! What do you want to do? The theater? Dinner? Something exotic? Vegetarian? Shall I come pick you up? Unless you'd rather go to the movies? An old Woody Allen movie? Polanski's latest?"

He doesn't dare look me in the face now.

"Adrien, do you like to play billiards?"

"I love the game!"

"Okay, come pick me up at nine. I live. . . ."

"I know where you live."

"Oh I see! And what else do you know?"

"Lots of things—top secret."

"That would surprise me. But go ahead anyway."

"You have two Siamese cats. You live with your father. You're going to enroll at Assas. You take dance on Tuesdays and Thursdays at the Marais center. I even went there one day, just to see you. You've never been in love and. . . ."

"And . . . who gave you such good information?"

"I have my informants. I hope you're not angry."

"Should I be?"

"I don't think so."

It worked—the dentist trick. Life can go on. Life is beautiful! How sweet it all is! What a good thing it was, after all, that mama was late! How I love him! Mama? What mama?

19

The last time she didn't come to meet me, I left her. Yes, the way you leave a lover: "It's over, I'm going." And that was the last separation—but maybe the most dramatic—in my life as a little girl.

I had just turned seven. It was a September afternoon like this one. She was supposed to come pick me up when school got out, not far away from here in the rue Saint-Benoît. She had promised to take me to see *Rox et Roucky* at the movies. Once again, I was so happy! All the children knew the song by heart and traded the stickers at recess.

By four-thirty, they had almost all gone home, running, in little bunches. By five, a few mamas were still gossiping on the sidewalk. They had brought bread and chocolate and were stroking their little kids' hair. As for me, I was still waiting, alone in front of the gate, my little cap pulled well down over my ears and my mittens deep in my pockets. It was beginning to rain. I said to myself: "She's late, but she's going to come. She promised me: She's going to come."

At five-fifteen, I start to worry: We'll miss the show!

At five-thirty, I panic and begin reciting my multiplication tables so as not to feel the time passing too much.

At eight times nine, I dissolve in tears: Mama isn't coming, mama won't come, something has happened to mama. . . .

I go home as fast as I can, like Speedy Gonzalez.

I climb the stairs four at a time: "Don't worry, mama, I'm here, I'm your little Louise, and I'm racing back. . . ."

It's six-thirty. Mama is here. She isn't in the least worried. She's in the bath listening to Françoise Hardy and chewing on some licorice. She had simply forgotten. Or her watch had stopped. Or she hadn't wanted to.

Dumbfounded, I don't listen to her explanations.

I can only repeat: "You promised! You promised!" And I run into my room swallowing my tears and taking good care to slam the door behind me with my foot, the way she does when she's really angry. "It calms me down," she says.

All it does is hurt my ankle.

I sit down at my little desk, sad, but also serious, determined to ask myself some basic questions this time: "Why is she so bad to me? What have I done to her? Not all mamas are like her, I know—why does my mama in particular forget me like that, listening to stupid music?"

My thumb in my mouth, in order to think better, I decide I've had enough and that papa, unlike mama, always keeps his promises.

At random I open a book that a friend of mama's gave me. Its title, *The Devil Inside You,* has always intrigued me. Even, I go; odd, I don't go. Page 166: "wonder." Six letters. Even. One more try. Page 74: "hot chocolate." Twelve letters. Even again. It's settled. Collect a few things. Pull a stool up to the wall telephone in the kitchen. Call papa: "I want you to come here and get me. I don't want to stay here anymore." And then, finally, go back to the living room.

Mama has come out of her bath and is draped in her yellow dressing gown. She's standing in front of her mirror putting black mascara on her eyelashes. I say to her: "Listen, I'm leaving." She looks at me without understanding and answers me, smiling: "There's a good movie on TV tonight, a western.

Would that be fun?" Then she sees the little suitcase at my feet, observes me for a long moment, sits down, lights a cigarette, shakes her pretty hair and in a hollow voice, simply repeats: "You are? You're leaving?"

I nod. My throat is full of tears. I would like to explain it to her: "Forgive me, mama, dear mama, I have to go. It's not really your fault, I miss papa." But I don't say anything. I don't *want* to say anything. I'm so afraid of bursting into tears. I'm making such an effort to seem grown-up and confident.

You must be strong, I tell myself. And I try to look at her as though she weren't my mama anymore, as though I had never seen her before: her full face, as healthy as a piece of fruit; those fine vertical lines around her mouth that I notice for the first time; her light eyes; the pale blue that I'm suddenly envious of; hey, she has plucked her eyebrows too much, it makes her look surprised. I would like to take her hand, get on her knees and snuggle up to her, the way I used to. But she would have to make a gesture, smile. She doesn't budge. Not a move, not a word, nothing. She has put her mascara down on the little dressing table, and she's waiting.

I tell myself she's going to cry, beg me to stay: "My baby, please forgive me, I love you, don't go." She doesn't move. Maybe she thinks it's better this way, or it won't change anything. Maybe she feels that, from the height of my seven years, I've made up my mind.

We remain frozen, face to face, for a long interval, blinking our eyes in the light.

She gives a tentative smile, which could be taken for encouragement. For a moment, I even have the feeling she's relieved that I'm going. The idea bowls me over and I catch myself taking a step toward her, a very little step—as though resentment and pain together were already making me regret what I'm about to do. But no! Her distress, her despair, which she isn't hiding now. . . . Again I'm about to cry, but I'm also reassured, and I settle into my determination and take up my little suitcase again. Your pretty pale face, mama. . . .

No longer knowing what to say, nor which feeling to opt for, I leave without turning back, as in the movies, or a song.

I pass in front of the wall of photos, the famous photos of the happy years, those cartoon images of a stillborn happiness. Dog-eared, yellowed photos, frozen smiles, faces hardly recognizable. Papa and you, as adolescents, at the edge of the Sivergues swimming pool. You holding me in your arms, when I was five or six months old, bald, and already so near-sighted, you called me "my little Buddha." Papa and you, again, in black and white, in front of the olive green Autobianchi convertible. All three of us, a little later, you two holding my hands in the Luxembourg Gardens: flowered shirts, striped caps and wedgies. That terrible, indecent gaiety. The temptation to tear them down, those photos, to trample them underfoot: "Lies! Lies! These pictures are lies!" But I only lower my eyes and continue on my way, my little suitcase heavier than I would have believed. Think! My stuffed animals, my red dress, my drawing notebooks.

I totter under the weight. Above all, don't let anything show. Stay nice and straight, stiff, in the narrow hallway. Walk like a jumping jack, or like a big girl, with a neat step, nice and distinct. Look one last time at the apartment I think I'll never see again. The canopied bed. The wax dummy, the green carpeting. A little sweat beads my temples. Come on, Louise, this is only a bad moment to get through. Aren't I almost eight years old? I think mama has never known how hard it was for me to leave her.

Papa, who is already waiting for me downstairs, doesn't ask any questions. He takes me by the hand. We are swallowed up in a taxi. "Papa, what exactly is a republic?" He looks at me, rather surprised. Then he sets out to explain the Right, the Left, Fascism, the revolution—anything, rather than the life that is ending, and the other life that is beginning.

My sorrow, afterward? Moderate. And rather quickly eclipsed by the happiness of living—at last—with papa. But now and then I was consumed by remorse, overcome by the feeling that in leaving her, I had helped her to destroy herself. For it was after I left that she began to go downhill. The appointments she doesn't keep anymore, the friends she avoids, her face, thinner now, the whole days she spends in bed, waiting for who knows what, smoking brown tobacco and counting the cracks in the ceiling. And then the photographers, the agencies that get fed up, the rumors that spread—you can't depend on Alice anymore, Alice isn't what she once was.

Please forgive me, mama. With all my heart I ask your forgiveness. You don't laugh anymore now. You hardly even wrinkle your nose anymore, when we're together again and make fun of some bigwig. Oh mama, I beg you, laugh, laugh again, laugh the way you used to. You know none of this is serious. You know I'm just an accident along the way. You were there so little of the time, weren't you? You ignored me so much. No, no, don't say anything. I know it. I bothered you. I was in the way. Did you ever take me to the doctor, take me on a suitable vacation, without catastrophes or melodramas, offer me advice? Did you ever listen to me? Understand me?

Yes, of course, it's mean. One doesn't judge a mother's love by these ordinary attentions. How right you are! And yet. . . .

We weren't made for each other, that's the truth. No, no, let me finish. You had more to do than just raise a daughter. I understand, I understand so well. It takes time, in the end, to mess up a life. It isn't so easy. It takes energy, and especially consistency.

"I don't agree, pet, no time to walk you to school, no time to teach you to swim, no time to make you happy. I have to kill myself, I have to sleep with a woman, I have to rob a house. Please forgive me, I'm busy bungling my life. You don't have a place in that wretchedness."

At the same time, we actually loved each other. Maybe we thought it was the thing to do, to love each other, mother and daughter. But still, we believed in it. With pain, awkwardness, worry, pain again, but we believed in it. And I, and I, despite what anyone might say to me, despite what people told me and what I forgot, despite our missed appointments, despite this rendezvous today, so similar in the end to so many other rendezvous you didn't come to either, despite everything, despite you, in the face of everyone, despite drugs and craziness, despair and prison, despite your egotism, your dreadful egotism, which is also a sin against yourself, despite your carelessness, despite your nonchalance, now that everything is over and the page has been turned, now that nothing more comes to me from you, except memories that take the place of tenderness and warmth, I would like you to know, mama, that I have loved you infinitely.

It's funny, really. You've given me such different things. A taste for pretty objects. The talent that has become so useful to me of never completely getting lost in the storms of the world. You've also given me a capacity for dazzling, and a desire to dazzle. But also—and how could I forget it? and why hide it?—the desire never, never to be like you. Mama, my mama, my absolute antimodel. There. That's the way it is. That's what we've come to.

I could explain it to you better, go deeper into the debt and the resentment. But what would be the good of that? Why go back over the harm you've done me, and what you've given me without even intending to? All that is so distant. I'm eighteen years old and it's so distant. I've been waiting for you since this morning and this time I'm not suffering.

You see, I think our only happy times were ones that I dreamed. I know them by heart. They were always the same ones. They were the times when I was in my bed waiting for the moment when I would have you all to myself, the way I used to. I knew you would come. All I had to do was decide. I was waiting for you, I was expecting you and you never disappointed me. You always came, light-hearted and lively and beautiful. You were there, close to me. I would take your hand, I would lead you with me into the night and at last I would talk to you the way I had never dared talk to you. I told you what I would never tell you now, I promised you what you wanted: "You'll see, mama, I'll come back, we'll live together again some day, we'll be happy, you'll see." I listened to a few notes of your laughter, I looked at your insolent beauty, your large eyes turned toward the light. You murmured to me that I was your child and that you loved me, that you would always love me. Your red hair flowed over your shoulders. We talked all night long, I felt good. And then, the morning would come. I would find myself there alone, turned to the wall, heavy with sorrow.

And it would begin again the next day, and the day after, ad infinitum. It was our only way of being together, of being happy together. You were right, mama, about your "illusion of happiness."

20

Mama will never come. Why should I go on with this farce? I know now that she will never come. Even the waiter knows it: It's his turn to go off duty, he's coming to collect for his huckleberry tart, his tea with vanilla, his coffees, he's the least kind of them all, he hardly looks at me. Even he has realized that mama won't come.

It's almost night. The shadows are

lengthening on the little square where they met once upon a time, twenty years ago. That could be Her. That could be Him. No, of course not. All that is over. It belongs to another time, another world. People are hurrying, all of a sudden. She would never hurry like that. Mama never hurries. I always knew, underneath, that she wasn't going to come. I waited all day long, but in my heart of hearts I knew it.

It isn't serious. It's a game. I'm going to leave too. And I'm going to hurry too. "Nine o'clock," he said with his smile full of promises. Nine o'clock. I'm so happy. Because he, at least, will come, I know it.

It isn't serious. It's been this way since the beginning. Once again, for the thousandth time, we had a rendezvous and we missed each other. Once again, for the thousandth time, like when I was little, when I would wait for the night and my dreams to be with you again, I've spent these hours seeing you and thinking about you. Do you know that I've seen more of you today than in eighteen years? Do you know that I've been closer to you, waiting for you, than if I had seen you? I'll always wait for you.

This is how I'll find you again.